SENATOR

POLITICS OF LOVE, BOOK 2

SIENNA SNOW

Copyright Page

Cover Design: Pink Ink Designs

Editor: Jennifer Haymore

www.siennasnow.com

ISBN - 978-1-948756-02-0 (eBook)

ISBN - 978-1-948756-03-7 (Print)

POLITICS OF LOVE, BOOK 2

ABOUT THE AUTHOR

Author Sienna Snow is a writer, mom, and world traveler, who plans to visit every continent within the next ten years.

She writes steamy romances, about strong and smart women, who choose to find love through atypical circumstances.

Sign up for her newsletter to be notified of releases, book sales, events and so much more.

www.SiennaSnow.com

authorsiennasnow@gmail.com

Goodreads

Facebook

Twitter

Instagram

BOOKS BY SIENNA SNOW

CHAPTER ONE

"JACINTA, I know he's your friend, but I still can't believe the citizens of Texas voted in a liberal as governor."

I smiled and held in a sarcastic retort as I glanced at my date for the Governor's Ball, Kevin Copula Stanton III. Kevin, of all people, should have known better than to insult the very man whose expensive alcohol and food he was enjoying in large quantities.

"He's a good guy. Just because he doesn't agree with you doesn't make him a liberal."

"Labeling himself as an Independent won't change what he is. His agenda speaks for itself." Kevin motioned to a passing waiter for a drink and continued. "His success is because of his war-hero POW status."

Visions of pulling every one of Kevin's immaculately groomed white-blond hairs out of his head popped into my mind.

"Be nice, Kevin," I warned. "I can't believe you'd talk shit about one of your closest friends."

His bright blue eyes twinkled with amusement, and I realized he'd suckered me with his words.

Bastard.

"I deserved that," I admitted.

"Well, I had to do something to get you to focus on me. Remember, we're pretending that we're a couple. Don't forget. There are eyes and ears everywhere."

"Sorry. I wish..." I trailed off.

"So do I, Jacinta. So do I. We'd make an unstoppable team." He fingered one of the curls sitting on my shoulder and then said with a smirk, "I think I'd make an exceptional first husband one day."

I studied Kevin, his good looks and athletic physique added in with his charm and charisma. He was the poster boy for conservative ideals and the perfect match for anyone with political aspirations. If only there were something more than friendship between us. Together, we were the image of Ken and Barbie in a modern Republican package.

The number of times the RNC chairman had told me having Kevin by my side would guarantee the party's nomination once I reached the age of qualification... What he didn't realize was that I was destined for the spot whether Kevin was with me or not. I was the face of the new Republican movement. A movement that leaned more centrist, appealing to a younger demographic, one that would keep the party alive and away from the verge of extinction as our current president had driven it.

I set my hand on Kevin's arm. "Let's make a deal."

"I'm all ears."

"If I haven't found Mr. Right in the next few months, I'll let you make an honest woman of me."

He kissed my forehead. "Do you promise?"

"I promise," I responded, kissed his cheek, and then said in a whisper, "but what happens if you decide the guy you're seeing is Mr. Right?"

A sadness passed through his eyes and disappeared just as fast when a photographer approached us for a photo.

"Smile pretty." He slipped his arm around my waist, and I leaned into him, posing for a few shots.

"Come on. We need to move toward your brothers. This way it'll look as if we're still mingling with conservatives. And be sure not to make any sudden movements, or the predators will smell fresh blood."

I laughed aloud—I couldn't help myself—and I knew it would draw attention, giving the perfect addition to the cover Kevin and I were trying to portray to the public. "You're too much. Come on."

Just when we were a few feet away from my twin brother, Tyler, a man with slicked-back black hair and gleaming white teeth stepped into our path.

I almost groaned but kept it inside.

Albert Walton. He was a staunch supporter of my former

opponent in the Texas Senate race, and his family was known to make considerable contributions to the party. No matter my personal feelings toward the man, I had to play nice.

"Jacinta." Albert kissed my cheek and then he turned. "Kevin." Albert shook Kevin's hand. "How are you two enjoying this extravagance?"

Not two seconds and there was an underhanded jab. What could I expect? I'd helped elect an enemy, and no one, especially not someone who voted only along strict party lines, was going to let me forget it.

When Kevin had made his comment, I'd known it was a joke. He and our new governor, Veer George, were old Air Force friends who enjoyed ribbing each other. Albert, on the other hand, couldn't get over the fact Veer had won the election by a three-to-one margin.

"It's quite tame compared to previous balls. Don't you remember the opera singer from a few years ago?" Kevin asked.

"I should know better than to say anything to you, Stanton. Especially since he's a former military buddy."

Neither Kevin nor I commented on Albert's statement.

"At least George had the decency to commemorate the Texas soldiers we lost in the recent firefight in North Africa." Albert motioned to the families of the fallen men and women who were mingling with the gala attendees.

"Veer is a decorated war hero who's used his personal funds to create an organization to help veterans. This isn't something new to him." I spoke my comment with a tone of annoyance that made it seem as if I thought Albert was an idiot. "His charities hold multiple events throughout the year for the families of all our fallen military."

Kevin cleared his throat and squeezed my waist, telling me to keep my cool. I had to remember, we weren't attending the ball as Veer's friends but as members of the Republican Party sizing up future opponents.

"He's a rich boy with money to blow. A trust-fund kid who decided to get into politics because he had nothing better to do."

I clenched my jaw, took the flute of champagne Kevin handed me from a passing waiter, and swallowed a healthy gulp.

Maybe if I numbed my senses, this dipshit who'd interrupted my evening wouldn't give me thoughts of killing him with my stilettos.

If there was a spoiled rich boy in the vicinity, it was Albert. He came from oil money and had never had to hold down a job in his life. The thought of forgoing his family's means and serving the nation was a foreign concept to him. He'd enjoyed a playboy lifestyle for most of his thirty-four years on Earth, going from one social gathering to the next. He would have continued his exploits if his father hadn't made him move into their family's business.

After a few seconds, the alcohol had taken a mild effect, and I was able to speak. "Albert, I understand you're still upset about last year's loss, but let's keep tonight pleasant. Remember, we're the face of the party, after all."

"I meant no offense, Jacinta. I never assumed you'd be so sensitive to any comments about Veer George. I'd expect sensitivity about your liberal sister-in-law, but George is just a friend of your family."

I flashed Albert a death glare and then moved my gaze across the room to where Samina Kumar-Camden stood with my older brother, Devin. They laughed, joked, and mingled with everyone around them.

God, I wished I were with them. They were my family and knew how to help me let go and enjoy myself. But I was working, and this was all about making an impression on the voters, specifically those with deep pockets.

Samina caught my stare. She cocked a brow at Kevin, since she found him sexy as sin, and then made a gagging gesture while pointing at Albert. Devin quickly stopped her and gave her a disapproving glare and then said something that had her frowning. I could imagine it had to be along the lines of telling her to behave. As the junior senator from Washington, she had to project a respectable image and not make fun of supporters of opposing parties.

I smiled. Samina had my back, even though we shared different political views.

I guessed I should take a cue from my best friend and sister-in-law.

"Albert." I patted his arm and then pointed at his wife, who looked lonely standing by herself in the corner of the room. "Let's call a truce for the night. I just made it home after a thirty-six-hour pointless filibuster by our liberal counterparts that went nowhere. I don't have the energy. And you've left your beautiful new wife all alone. Go tend to her."

"I hear you, Jacinta." Albert gave me an authentic smile, kissed my cheek, nodded at Kevin, and turned in the direction of his wife.

"That was impressive. You went from pissed-off viper to charming socialite in a matter of seconds."

"Whatever." I nudged Kevin. "One thing I can say is that all of those cotillion classes Carol Camden forced me to take as a child came in handy tonight. Nothing like a smile to hide thoughts of murder."

"I'm not so sure learning the correct knives and forks to use or how to ballroom dance did me any good." Kevin frowned. "I'm still more at home in the woods with an open fire, a cold beer, and my rifle."

"So speaks the man with a chain of five-star hotels around the world."

"Shh. That's a secret."

"You're such a goofball. Come on, before someone else interrupts us."

TWO HOURS LATER, I MADE MY WAY OUT OF THE ladies' room and down the hall to where Kevin waited for me. After I'd calmed my ire at Albert and he left to tend his wife, the evening continued with mingling and charming the "old-school money men" as my dad liked to call them, something I'd learned how to do from the time I was in diapers.

As the daughter of Senate Majority Leader and ultra-conservative Louisiana Senator Richard Camden, I'd spent my childhood interacting with the very men whose deep pockets I needed to tap into. I was part of the fourth generation of politicians coming out of Louisiana and Texas.

When I'd come onto the political scene, it had been a challenge getting anyone to see past the pretty face I'd inherited from my gorgeous mother. I was expected to become a debutante, marry young to an up-and-coming Southern businessman, and produce the next crop of conservative children. Thankfully my parents never pushed the status quo on me. They'd recognized I wasn't cut out for the path my mother had chosen. As a senator's wife, she worked hard, sometimes too hard, and she was happy letting my father take the lead. I, on the other hand, was never going to let my dreams come second to my man's.

The one I'd end up with would see the intelligence and drive under the perfectly groomed package.

I smiled and tucked my purse under my arm, continuing down the endless hall that led to the ballroom.

I still remembered the day my father found me doing Calculus BC homework for my brother Devin, who was a high school senior. At first, Dad thought I was a silly twelve-year-old messing around, but then he realized I was correcting Devin's mistakes.

He'd been so shocked by my abilities that he'd sat dumbfounded and at a loss for words, and Dad never was short on words. Once he'd recovered, he'd picked me up, twirled me around, and then told me I was going to one day hold the highest office in the country. What he hadn't known was that I'd had the same plan for myself since I was eight, and the then-sitting president had made a snide comment about women knowing their place in the world. As a young girl, I had no idea I'd heard the comment out of context or that the president was a huge advocate for women's rights—all I knew was I would be taking his job one day.

"Hey, you. Are you ready to blow this popsicle stand?" Kevin asked as he approached me seconds after I reentered the ballroom. "It's nearly one in the morning, and we still have to go through some logistics for upcoming events."

His words triggered a yawn, and I covered my mouth with my hand. "The thought of finances, budgets, and fundraising sounds too exhausting for tonight. Can we skip it?"

Kevin tucked my arm under his and walked me toward where Samina and our friends stood. The late hour had caused the room to clear to half its previous capacity, making it easier to enjoy a few moments with the people who mattered.

"No, one of us will be on a plane Monday morning since Senate is in session, and the other has to run his family's businesses."

"Fine, I guess we both have to be adults tonight." I frowned. "You spoil all my fun."

At that moment, a voice I'd rather never encounter again in my life spoke.

"Hello, Ms. Camden. It's good to see the woman who stole my job."

I stiffened but kept my face emotionless.

Before I could respond, Grey Decker, former senator from Texas, gripped my hand in a painful hold. His gaze, filled with hate and anger, bored into me.

If anyone should have had a visceral reaction, it was me. This man thought he could ruin my reputation and those of countless others in his quest for political status. I would never regret unseating the bastard.

"It's not stealing if sixty-five percent of the voters wanted me to represent the party," I said and dug my nails into his palm, resulting in a wince and him releasing my hand.

I was not going to let this man see how much his touch made my skin crawl or that he held any power over me from what he had helped his son do to me.

"I heard the president wanted you to join one of his advisory committees, but you declined." His words were slurred, telling me he'd indulged in more than a few drinks. "Guess it was too much heat for you to handle as a junior senator. You should have left the hard work to those of us who have experience."

Was this his version of polite interaction? If he wanted to play, I'd play. Fucker.

"Was there a question in your statement, or do you enjoy hearing yourself speak?" I took a sip of my drink and gave him my politician smile. The one I'd perfected to keep from giving away any of my true feelings. The one I had to learn over the years from dealing with men like him to reach my position.

"Look here, little girl. I know what you and your—"

"Hello, Grey." Kevin cut off Decker before he could make a scene, stepping between Decker and me.

I loved Kevin so much. He knew little of my history with the former Texas senator, except that I hated Grey Decker with a passion. And because Kevin was a friend, he never pushed me to reveal my deep-seated feelings.

"I heard you're about to become a grandfather. How is Cara doing?" Kevin asked, referring to Decker's very pregnant daughter.

Decker ignored Kevin's question and kept his focus on me. "I'd be careful dating this piranha. She'll eat you for political gain."

I laughed aloud, making sure the people around me saw the winner of the most contentious election in Texas history enjoying her time with her former opponent.

Last year's election had caused a huge rift in the party with people taking sides. The old school tended to follow Decker, but the progressive Republicans and the younger members of the party fell behind me. In the end, I'd garnered enough votes to gain the party's nomination and then I'd defeated my Democratic opponent by a landslide.

"Grey, let me make this clear. The election is over. I won. Get over it."

"How dare you. When I'm done with you, you won't have a pot to piss in."

"Grey." Kevin's voice took on a tone I rarely heard, one

that vibrated with authority. The one I'm sure scared the shit out of his subordinates when he was in the Air Force. "It's time you moved on. You are crossing a line that will not bode well for you."

"Now you're threatening me?"

"No, it isn't a threat, it's a promise. Your money can't cover up your or your son's improprieties. After last year, I'd assumed you would have learned your lesson. I guess I was wrong."

"You're a traitor to conservative values, Stanton."

"Hello, everyone." Veer George confidently approached us in the way he always maneuvered through a room. He stepped in between Decker and me, making Decker move out of his way, something the former senator couldn't mistake for anything but a slight. "I thought I'd come over to see how you've enjoyed the party."

Veer Kiran George, the first Independent governor of Texas in the modern era, was a sight for sore eyes. Women always took a double-take when he entered the room. He wasn't handsome in the traditional sense, but in a bad-boy way that made one think of all the trouble he could get you into.

Tonight, he'd dressed in a tailored suit, custom made to accommodate his towering height and the chiseled form underneath. The jet-black hair he usually wore in a messy style was slicked back in the image of a Bollywood movie star. The stubble on his jaw that I knew he hadn't shaved on purpose, combined with the scar running along the right side of his face, gave him an almost rakish, piratical look. He oozed sex appeal, making me have visions of fanning my lady parts.

"Hello, Jaci." Veer kissed my cheek, lingering for a second longer than was appropriate.

My stomach jumped as I inhaled the rich spice of his cologne.

As he pulled back, he greeted Kevin, all but ignoring Decker.

Decker had questioned Veer's military record a few years ago, and Veer had never gotten over it. If there was something Veer George took pride in, it was his service in the Air Force.

"How is everyone? Are you enjoying the evening?" Veer searched my eyes, motioning with his chin toward Decker and asking if I was okay.

I gave a slight inclination of my head. I would never let Decker see how much I wished he'd fall off the nearest cliff.

Very few people knew everything I'd endured to become the darling of the conservative movement. Veer happened to be one of them.

Politics was brutal, but if you were a female, it was twice as hard. Those in positions of power would use their pull to shame and intimidate to keep their opponents in check.

"This evening has been lovely. I'm so glad you were able to convince Sam and Devin to come down," I said, glancing behind him to my family. "Are we still on for the cookout?"

He flashed me a wicked grin, sending a shiver down my spine. This man was too good looking to be a politician. When he stared at me the way he was right now, all I could think of was what he'd look like naked with only his bowtie fastened to his neck.

Besides his sexy-as-sin body and face, he was the son of a technology and real estate mogul. Veer had decided to serve the country his father had immigrated to before Veer's birth instead of taking over a billion-dollar company.

He believed in paying things forward, and enlisting in the Air Force was his way of showing his appreciation for a country that had afforded his family such great success.

"Only if Kevin promises not to do anything behind the grill."

"I only burned the burgers one time. It wasn't as if I planned for the insurgents to attempt an attack on the base."

Before the lighthearted conversation could go any further, Grey decided it was the opportune time to interject his presence again and said to Kevin and me, loudly enough for everyone around us to hear, "Isn't it inappropriate for the two of you to fraternize with those who don't hold our moral standards? The voters are going to see you for the liars you are."

I groaned and saw a twitch pulse on the sides of both Veer's and Kevin's jaws.

"Grey, I think you need to lay off the alcohol. You are a guest in my home and attacking Jacinta and Kevin, two of my closest friends, will only make you look the fool." Veer's gaze bored into Decker's. "Remember when you said all's fair in politics? You're the one who hired someone to destroy the reputation of Samina Kumar-Camden, a person I consider family. Jacinta only used the information to expose you for a fraud and not the morally high standard man you pretend to portray."

He motioned to someone who then approached Decker and escorted him away from us.

"If you'll excuse me." Veer took my hand in his, kissing my knuckles. "I'll see you later, much later. Enjoy your evening." He nodded to Kevin, who inclined his head, then walked into the crowd of guests.

"He wants in your pants, like yesterday," Kevin said. "And from the look on your face, I'd say the feeling's mutual."

"It's complicated." I sighed. "If only it didn't have such a big price."

"The best things never come easy, Jaci."

CHAPTER TWO

AROUND THREE IN THE MORNING, after strategizing with Kevin at his hotel room for what felt like days, he dropped me off at home. We were both exhausted and desperate for some sleep before all of our friends invaded my house for a weekend house party. Finances, budgets, and planning were all part of the road Kevin and I had joined together to follow. I just sometimes wished I could take a break from it all.

I dragged myself up the steps of the hundred-and-twenty-year-old Victorian mansion my mother had given me when I'd decided to move to Texas after law school.

My mother was the eldest daughter of a Texas oil billionaire, who had inherited the large Austin estate and a sizeable trust fund following my grandfather's death. No matter how much she loved the beautiful historic home, she rarely used it. Dad's schedule kept both my parents too busy to get away for more than a few days, and the travel from New Orleans, where my parents' home was, to Austin was too long to endure and keep up the pace of their lives.

Lucky for me, I loved living in Texas, especially Austin, and therefore out of all my siblings, I was the person to get the house.

I nodded to my security team, giving the signal I was in for the night, then settled inside the house and closed the door behind me. I set my keys and purse on the giant quartz island in the middle of my kitchen, leaning against it for a moment to enjoy the silence. Politics meant I was always on; quiet moments were rare.

Turning, I kicked off my shoes in the middle of the hallway and began stripping out of my dress and pulling off my false lashes. My mother would probably have a thing or two to say about throwing my clothes around, but I was too dead tired to give a shit about proper dispensing of dirty laundry.

God, I hated events like tonight's where the people I wanted to spend my time with were at a distance, and the ones I had to associate with were royal pains in the ass and full of themselves. Kevin was the exception. Without him, I wasn't sure I'd have survived.

I couldn't lie and say what I'd suggested to him about marriage was something I wasn't serious about. He was a catch and everything I'd want in a man. Except the fact we both pined for men we couldn't keep. No matter how far the party had come, an openly gay man had a limited future. To those who held old-school views, it wouldn't matter that Kevin was a decorated war hero or that he'd spent years serving in the Air Force. All that would matter was that he was gay.

He deserved so much better. But I couldn't force him to do anything he wasn't ready to do.

If we continued on the path we were on, we'd have no choice but to announce our engagement in the next year.

I knew thinking this was selfish to the greatest degree, but if authentic love wasn't in the cards for us, at least I'd have my dear friend by my side in the political chess match I'd decided to play as an eight-year-old.

Turing on the shower, I waited until the water was at my desired temperature and stepped inside, letting the scalding spray seep into my skin.

Was it possible to have the dream and the man I wanted?

Nope. The White House comes at a price. Marriage to one of your closest friends but a lonely bed and watching the man you love live a life with someone else.

I shook the cryptic thought from my head. I knew what I had to do. Now it was time to do it.

My only problem was I couldn't be positive I'd be able to go through with it when the time came.

I cupped the back of my neck and closed my eyes, picturing beautiful hazel ones gazing at me.

Veer.

I should have known he would be my doom from the weekend so long ago when Samina had brought her brother, Ashur, and his best friend, Veer, to visit my family in New Orleans. Both men had barely returned home from their first tour in Afghanistan and were going to meet up with Kevin, an Air Force buddy, and Devin, who'd attended Harvard with them.

Veer had had this quiet, brooding sense about him that told me he'd seen more than he'd ever admit. Over the course of those days, I'd gotten my first experience of Veer's underlying appeal and my initial ideas of how he'd make the kind of politician people could stand behind.

It wasn't until almost ten years later that he'd succumbed to my nagging and entered the race.

Now, he was everything I'd envisioned him becoming as the new governor of Texas. He'd endeared himself to a population who in other times would never have voted for him. In the year he'd held office, he'd kept every promise he'd made. Rumors were swirling that he was the next viable candidate to challenge the sitting president.

Reaching over to a recessed shelf, I grabbed a bottle, poured some soap onto my loofah, and washed my body.

God, please don't make it happen so soon.

I wasn't sure how I'd handle having him as my opponent. And I knew with little doubt that he'd win and unseat our current president. Then I'd have to be the challenger to the very man I'd pushed into politics.

As the last of the suds cascaded down my body, I leaned my forehead against the warmed tile of the shower.

I couldn't jump ahead of myself—nothing was a given. I'd learned that numerous times since I'd entered the world of politics.

The door opened behind me, causing my breath to hitch and my skin to prickle with awareness. There was only one person who could get past my security. The man who'd hired them.

"What are you doing here? Aren't you worried someone might have seen you leave the mansion for my house?."

"No." Strong golden arms caged me against the wall, and crisp hair grazed my back. "Keep your hands right there and spread your legs."

I instinctively listened, resulting in a hum of approval along my neck and the feel of firm thighs pressing against my separated ones.

"I missed you," I gasped out.

He snorted and then said against my ear, "I want you to know if that prick ever tries to touch what's mine, I will break every one of his fingers."

His possessive tone sent a wave of arousal throughout my body. I wasn't the type of woman who was ever comfortable with dominant men, but for some reason, with this one, I just about purred whenever his caveman side appeared.

"Did you forget that you're the one who wanted me to date Kevin?"

Kevin's secret was something I'd never disclose to anyone, even my lover.

"That was before us, and I wasn't talking about him, and you know it," he bit out, making me cringe inside.

"Don't go there. The last thing I want to do is think

about Decker. He's not worth it. Besides, you had him escorted out."

He grunted. "I'd rather have put my fist through his face, but I knew you wouldn't want that kind of attention, so I restrained myself."

"I didn't know I had that kind of power over you, Governor George," I whispered.

He cupped my breast and pinched the tip, causing a low guttural moan to escape my lips.

"Veer."

He ignored my gasp of need and continued with our conversation. "I did run for the highest office in the state because of you."

I pushed back, but he barely budged. "That's bullshit, and you know it. I may have put the idea in your head, but nothing and no one makes Governor George do anything he doesn't want to."

He moved to my other nipple, gripping the nub in an almost painful squeeze that made my clit throb.

"Harder."

"Then explain to me why I've accepted the fact one of my closest friends is standing by your side and not me. You should have been with me years ago when we began, but you refused. You're mine, and I can't tell a single soul about it. Do you think I don't know that you're planning a future without me?"

My lips trembled. His words were a truth we avoided at all costs.

"It isn't that simple. We both have careers on the line."

"Do you think I give a fuck about my career?"

I let the feel of his hands on my chest and the heat of his skin on my back engulf my senses and pushed back the uneasiness that filled me whenever I thought about life without him.

"I give a fuck. We've sacrificed so much."

Veer cupped my jaw. "That's always been your problem. Everything comes second to your ambition. Especially me."

I couldn't deny his accusation. I had goals that would shatter if it came out that Veer and I were together. I'd never get the ultra-conservative vote if anyone knew I was in love with the Independent governor who leaned toward the liberal side.

"Veer, please," I pled. "I don't want to have this argument right now."

"Then what do you want to do?" His hand freed my face and moved down my body, across my stomach, and to my swollen folds.

My head fell back onto his shoulders. "I'm dying. It's been over a month since we've been together."

"Spell it out for me." He bit my earlobe as his fingers pushed through my cleft.

A large bulge pressed to my lower spine, making me have visions of dropping to my knees and engulfing him in my mouth.

"I can't hear you. I want you to be crystal clear," he said, plunging two fingers deep inside my sopping pussy.

I cried out, "You. I want you to fuck me."

"That's the plan." He pumped his digits as he strummed my aching nub with his thumb. "But I need you to come first."

Yes. There was nothing like his touch. He held a part of me no other man ever would.

I reached behind me to grab Veer's hair, but a low growl stopped me.

"Keep your hands where I ordered you to. I'm not kissing you until I'm ready."

"Veer," I whimpered but followed his command and returned my palms to the tile.

He knew how much I enjoyed his kisses. They were all-consuming and arousing to the point I could come from the glide of his tongue against mine.

He was hurting because we knew what was going to happen sooner rather than later.

I dropped my head forward, letting a tear fall and melt into the water streaming down my cheeks.

"No, baby." He tilted my face to him and said, "No thinking about anything but what's happening right now. Enjoy the pleasure only I can give you." And then, he sealed our lips.

We ate each other's mouths, tasting, sucking, savoring, as he played my aching sex with his masterful fingers.

My pussy quivered and flooded with arousal, and my already aching nipples budded to even harder points.

"Oh God. Veer. I can't hold on any longer."

"I know, love. I've got you." His arm came around my waist to hold me to him.

I rode his pistoning hand, and my swollen cleft clenched around him with each push and pull.

"Come now."

My body responded with spasms that made my mind cloud and ecstasy fill every cell in my being. Before I could come down from my bliss, he pulled out of me and replaced his finger with the head of his engorged cock.

"Yes," I moaned, pushing down until he was to the hilt. The girth of his erection left a pleasurable sting I craved whenever we were apart for any length of time.

He stilled his movement, letting me become accustomed to him.

"Let me know when you're ready." His voice was hoarse, laced with his own desire.

"I'm ready. Fuck me already."

"So demanding." He laughed into my hair, pulling out until he was at the crest of his long, thick cock, and then plunged balls-deep. "I guess you're okay with me having my wicked way with you."

I lifted up onto my tiptoes and tried to take over the pace, but I was too short.

"If you don't fuck me, I'm getting out of this shower and leaving you with a case of blue balls."

He shifted and rolled his hips in the way that drove me crazy.

"You were saying?"

I shook my head. "Nothing. Please don't stop."

"I wasn't planning on it. Now hold on and enjoy the ride." He pulled out and slammed back in.

We both cried out at the exquisite sensation. Veer fucked me hard, not wavering on his pace. His hand cupped my throat as the other molded my waist to him. I held on to his neck and pushed against the wall, unable to gain any leverage. I took what he had to give me.

There was nothing but the two of us here, no dueling careers or political aspirations or media. We were raw, and all we wanted was to sate the need we'd built over the past few weeks apart.

My body snapped and my orgasm cascaded around his thrusting cock. I screamed out Veer's name as he groaned against the clamping of my pulsing pussy.

Veer gripped my hair in a stinging hold, pulling my head back, and captured my mouth, drinking the remainder of my release from my lips. And then a few seconds later, he clenched his jaw as his orgasm erupted, and he pumped jets of hot semen deep into my soaking heat.

"I love you," he wheezed out, bracing us against the shower wall.

I responded without hesitation. "I love you."

We remained motionless, except for our panting breaths and the lingering pulse of his now softening cock.

After a minute or two, I looked over my shoulder and said, "We should get some sleep before the caterers arrive. Thank God it's only going to be our closest friends this weekend. I don't think I can do the pretend thing after tonight."

He gave me a tight smile, pulling from my body, and

then grabbed a bottle from the shelf, pouring a quarter-sized amount of shampoo into his hands. He turned me to face him, gathered my wet hair, and began to massage the sudsy liquid onto my scalp.

"What was that look for?" I asked, bracing my hands on his shoulders.

Veer rubbed harder but kept quiet.

Shit, he only went silent like this when I'd hurt him, and it seemed like that was all I ever did over the last few months.

"Veer." I placed a hand on his.

"Jaci, drop it unless you want to hear the truth."

He tilted my head under the cascading stream, working the shampoo away.

I wiped at the water in my eyes and glared at him.

"What is that supposed to mean?"

"You know exactly what I mean." He began to lather his hair and then rinsed, ignoring me.

As soon as he was soap free, he opened the door to the shower and stepped out, grabbing a towel from the rack and wrapping it around his waist.

I shut off the water in a huff and followed behind him, jerking my robe from the hook on the wall and shrugging it on.

"Dammit, Veer. What do you want from me?" I pushed my wet hair out of my eyes. "I'm trying. I..."

Before I could finish my sentence, he had me pushed against the bathroom wall.

His face was a play of pain and fury. "You want to

know what I want? I want to get married. I want to have children. I'm fucking thirty-five, and the woman I love refuses to marry me. What the hell do you think I want from you?"

He released me just as fast and walked out of the room.

CHAPTER THREE

Around six thirty in the morning, I woke, freshened up, and came down the steps leading to my kitchen. I yawned, trying to shake the last of my sleep from my mind. After Veer's abrupt departure from the shower, we spent the remainder of the night wrapped in each other's arms, doing everything to avoid the turmoil boiling between us, which meant we spent the night making love and losing ourselves in passion.

I moved toward the water kettle on the counter and set it to boil. Veer hadn't started the coffee, telling me he'd probably spent the morning reviewing the real estate and technology endeavors he'd had to step away from when he'd taken his oath as governor.

I'd felt Veer leave my bed a little over an hour earlier. For some reason, the man rarely if ever slept past five. It was something I'd had the hardest time getting used to when we'd first started our affair. I wasn't a late sleeper but waking at five every morning was too much for me to handle.

I picked up the French press, filled it to my desired level of Costa Rican coffee, and poured in the boiling water.

A newspaper sat on the counter, and I skimmed it as I waited for the rich brew to soak in all its flavors.

The headline read: "Texas Governor Opposes President's Budget Plan."

I shook my head, setting the paper back down, and poured two cups of coffee.

Veer had definitely disturbed a hornet's nest when he'd called out President Henry Edgar's budget plan. It wasn't as if Veer's views were unfounded—the president needed to revise his plan to encompass projects outside of his agenda. The issue was Veer had taken an aggressive stance against a conservative president in a conservative state, showcasing his liberal tendencies. Veer wasn't playing politics, and there was a chance people would remember he was a liberal-leaning Independent during the next election and vote him out.

With cups in tow, I stepped out of the patio doors and onto the deck.

Veer sat relaxed on a deck chair, watching the river. There was a deep intensity in his gaze that made my throat burn.

God he was sexy. There was a rough, untamed aura about him that let anyone know he would kick someone's ass if they ever thought to hurt the ones he loved. Up until he entered politics, he'd spent more time in military clothing and casual wear than in a suit. Although I could never complain about how he filled out a suit. Especially since I knew firsthand the hard, sculpted body underneath the tailored material.

Veer rubbed the scar that marred his gorgeous face. The one he'd received while on a mission in the Air Force. Seven years hadn't eased the pain I knew he felt whenever he clenched his jaw too tight. It was usually as a result of something I'd done. I had a way of getting under the skin of the man with a reputation for keeping his cool no matter the situation.

Veer looked up as I approached him. Without saying a word, he grabbed both cups, setting them on the small table beside him, and pulled me onto his lap.

"Couldn't find something else to wear in that giant closet of yours except for my shirt from last night?" He thumbed the lapel of the button-down cotton as his other hand crept up my leg to cup my ass.

"It smells like you."

He smirked. "Only you would find my used clothing appealing."

"If you only knew," I muttered.

Women threw themselves at him right and left. Most of the time he'd pretend he hadn't noticed the incessant flirting, but other times he'd smile, flirt back, and then politely excuse himself. Those were the moments when it grated on my nerves that the public had no idea we were a couple.

No, we were more than a couple. Veer was the only person outside of Samina that I could confide in about all the shit I had to wade through in my quest for the White House. Many of my political views clashed with his, but he'd never dismiss them. Instead, he'd debate his point so I would know how to handle anyone who would oppose my position.

"Can I ask you something?" I asked as I leaned against his chest.

Veer lifted a brow. "When have you ever needed permission to ask me anything?"

"Hardy, har, har. I'm being serious here. Why are you so vocal about the president's budget? Aren't you afraid you'll alienate the voters?"

"It's a bad deal all around. He thinks he's playing Monopoly and trying to buy out all the high-dollar places. What he doesn't see is that the money he's spending is real and belongs to the people of the country, including those who aren't in his income bracket. Don't tell me you support him?"

I lifted my head and frowned. "I told you over the phone last week what I thought. He's cutting the wrong things and spending in areas that will only cause ridiculous amounts of debt."

"Then why'd you ask?"

"Because you've been making a lot of headlines lately, and I always assumed you'd hold back some of your aggressive views until you were in office a little longer."

He smirked and then offered me his hand. "Hi, I'm

Veer George. Have we met before? Because I'm not sure if you know this about me, but I hate bullshit. My good looks weren't the only reason the voters elected me."

I couldn't help it—I laughed, pushing his arm down. "No, it was your hot bod."

"The only person who sees my body is you." He squeezed my hip, making me squirm. "And I better be the only one who sees yours."

"Possessive much?"

He cupped my cheek and stared into my eyes. "You have no idea."

The lighthearted mood immediately shifted, and a wave of uneasiness surrounded us.

We watched each other for another few seconds before Veer spoke. "I'm sorry about last night. I shouldn't have taken it out on you. I've missed you."

I couldn't let him take the blame; it was something that had been lingering between us for too long.

"It had to be said. But..." I nuzzled my face against his palm, "...I'm not ready for this to end."

His other hand flexed against my panty-covered bottom, and he sighed. "I went into this knowing we could never have a future, but I fell for you and made plans anyway."

"Don't you think it is the same for me? It wasn't supposed to go past that one night in Vegas. But neither of us could get enough of each other."

"Do you know how much I pray that your birth control fails and you have no choice but to marry me?"

I'd wished the same thing, so many times. I wanted the choice taken from me, but I couldn't do it. I wouldn't use my child as an excuse to give up what I wanted, what I'd worked so hard to achieve.

"Jaci, this won't work for much longer. I have plans, and either you're with me or you're not."

I frowned, pulling back from the comfort of his touch. "Is that an ultimatum, Veer Kiran George?"

He tugged my knee across his lap so I was straddling him.

"It's a fact. I want things you aren't willing to give me."

Despite what I'd said only moments earlier, I couldn't listen. Logic and emotions waged a battle inside me, and the last thing I wanted to do was accept what had to happen.

"I don't want to go there. I'm only home for a few days."

"When is the time to go there? Burying your head in the sand isn't going to change the facts." He gripped the back of my head and tilted my head up so I could stare into his beautiful hazel eyes. "Tell me you don't want to see where a future together goes."

"Of course, I do. But it could cost us everything."

A crease formed between his dark brows. "As I said, I don't give two shits about what it costs."

I smoothed my thumb over the crease and then shook my head and countered with, "As I said, I care."

He closed his eyes, dropping his head against the back of the armchair. His fingers flexed under my nape.

I knew I was selfish, but I wanted to prolong my time with the love of my life for a little longer. If things had been different and I wasn't so close to achieving my dreams, I might have thrown caution to the wind and jumped headfirst into everything that went with a relationship with Veer.

I loved his family as much as he loved mine. We were perfect for each other. Well, with the exception of our political affiliation, which had become the crux of our relationship. As the face of the reviving conservative movement, I'd lose any chance of the party's nomination in four years if I was with Veer. No matter what people openly said, the way they voted was an altogether different thing.

"Please," I whispered. "I don't want to fight. I want to enjoy the little time I have with you."

I covered the hand on my hip with mine and pushed him upward, under my shirt until he reached the lower curve of my breast. I squeezed his fingers around my swelling mound.

"Wait a little longer." I leaned down and grazed my lips over his. "For me, Veer."

"Jaci, what are you doing to me?"

"I'm seducing you, Governor George." I nipped his mouth again and rocked my cleft against his hardening cock.

He stopped my movement and peered into my eyes. "Damn you. No matter how much I want to end this to save us even more heartache, I can't do it. I need you too much." He pushed back from the chair, lifting me in his arms and wrapping my legs around his waist.

I grabbed on to his shoulders as he carried me inside the house.

"Veer, we can't go upstairs now. The caterers will be here soon and so will Sam and Devin."

He ignored my protests and took the stairs two at a time, not even considering the fact he had another human in his arms. This man's physical strength always took my breath away.

When we stepped onto the landing, instead of going toward my bedroom, he reached behind a set of curtains and pulled a lever. A door opened up, and he took another set of stairs that led to a rooftop deck.

The rooftop was my hideaway. A place to escape the world when things became too tough. I'd come up here as a kid with my grandmother. She'd tell me it was the perfect spot to spy on everyone around me while keeping others from seeing me.

Only my family and Veer knew it even existed. The number of times we'd spent the days making love and lounging away the hours were too numerous to count. The angle of the roof line and the positioning of the deck made it impossible for anyone around us to know anything that went on here.

And from the look in Veer's eyes, he was going to make use of the privacy.

"Veer, are you seriously planning to fuck me here when we're about to have a house full of guests?"

"Yep." He grinned as he set me on a daybed I had positioned against a wall. "I've done it before. Why not today? Besides, Sam and Devin are probably going to stop at their cabin before making it up to the house."

My brother Devin had a simple log cabin on the property along the river. It was the original house my great-grandparents had built before they'd made their money in oil. The cabin was Devin's special place, as this deck was mine. Since he moved to Washington State, he'd had very little time to come down to Austin and enjoy the seclusion of this property. Plus, now with Sam's political career, visits were even less frequent.

"They have DJ with them. I doubt sex is on their minds."

"Wrong again. DJ was dropped off with your mom and dad in New Orleans a few hours ago."

I frowned. "How do you know this?"

"I had a chat with Sam before you came out onto the patio. She wanted to let me know they were on their way."

"That still doesn't give us much time."

"Sure it does. Now, I suggest that you stop talking and start stripping," Veer said, stepping away from me and pulling his T-shirt over his head.

I nearly swallowed my tongue seeing his sculpted body. God, he was beautiful. He was built like an MMA fighter, all lean muscles and ropes of defined abs that lead to a sexy "v" trailing down under his pants. There was a light dusting of hair on his chest that made me want to reach out and run my fingers across his pecs.

I hummed my appreciation, and he gave me a shy smile in response. "Are you blushing, Governor George?"

"Indian people don't blush." He came toward me, yanking my legs out from under me and toward him.

He set one knee on the bed and then his strong arms pressed into the cushion beside my head, caging me.

"I beg to differ." I gripped his shoulders, lifting myself up, and smiled as he scowled. "You blush whenever I ogle your hot body."

"Jaci," he said, biting my lower lip. "Shut up and let me make love to you."

He kissed me in the way that turned my mind to mush. Our tongues glided along each other, licking, sucking, and savoring. His taste was intoxicating. I couldn't get enough.

My nails skimmed along the hard surface of his toned arms as my core became slick with need. I shifted my legs, wrapping one around his waist, and tried to draw him into me. I was desperate for the feel of his body against mine.

But instead of following through with my unsaid request, he broke our kiss.

I whimpered, "Veer."

"Shh. I want my breakfast." He slid down my body. His mouth moved down my throat, along the open collar of the shirt I wore. He took his time unbuttoning the fabric and exposing my skin. His lips surrounded my nipple, and he sucked, biting the tip and leaving a mix of pleasure-pain. He followed the same delicious torture on the other breast before moving lower.

His hand pushed between my legs and brushed against

the seam of my soaking pussy lips. He rubbed my arousal back and forth, increasing the ache deep inside my core. I arched up as a tingle shot through me, and I cried out.

He knew how to touch me, how to make me want nothing but him.

He settled between my legs, pushing them apart and resting them on his shoulders. His fingers held me open to him, exposing me to his gaze. He nuzzled into my slit, inhaling my scent, and then followed the action with a swipe of his glorious tongue.

"You always taste incredible." He pressed between my cleft, circling my swelling clit. "Do you know what it's like to crave you and not have you anywhere near me? A man could go insane for wanting you."

I gripped his hair in a fierce hold. "You have me. You're the only one who does."

In the next second his mouth was on me, feasting and fucking me with flicks and shallow plunges. My senses screamed with the need for release.

I cried out, "Oh God."

The rhythm of his mouth pushed me into a spiral, and I started coming. My pussy gushed and clenched. I couldn't breathe. This man consumed every thought in my mind.

He rubbed my cleft as he ravenously ate at me and had me flowing into a mind-blowing orgasm.

He crawled over me a few seconds later, and I felt the hot skin of his body press on mine. His hard, pulsing cock pushed between the lips of my sex, stretching me and filling me to the brim.

"Veer. I wish…" The feel of him was more than I could take and something I could never get enough of.

I wasn't ashamed of him. I wished to the bottom of my heart that it could be different, freer, but there was so much at stake, so much that could ruin our futures.

"I know baby, I know." He captured my hands, pinning them above my head, and stared into my eyes. "Stop thinking. Focus on the feel of my cock pummeling your tight pussy."

We watched each other as he drove into me over and over.

I loved this man more than I could have ever imagined loving someone. He was mine. Well, at least for now.

"I said stop thinking."

My lips trembled, and I nodded, my head rising to capture his lips.

My core quivered and then clenched, fisting him in a tight grip, as another orgasm washed over me. I tore free from his mouth, screaming my release and pushing Veer into his.

He groaned my name, coming in hard shudders, and said, "I can't let you go. Not yet."

CHAPTER FOUR

Two HOURS after my mind-blowing sex session with Veer, I leaned against my kitchen counter and drank down a strong martini. The olive-infused concoction burned down my throat and warmed my stomach.

Veer had left in much the same way as he'd come in the night before. I hated that no one outside my circle was supposed to know we were together. He'd accepted how it had to be, reluctantly, but he'd accepted.

Now I stood in my kitchen with guilt weighing down on me. I should set Veer free and let him move on. But I couldn't do it. If I did, it would mean I'd lost my one opportunity to be with the love of my life.

"So, are you going to tell me what's going on between Veer and you or am I going to have to guess?"

I stared at my beautiful best friend and sister-in-law, Samina Kumar-Camden. She was a world-renowned celebrity attorney-turned-junior senator from Washington

State. She also happened to have known me long enough to recognize when I was in a brooding kind of mood.

I'd tried to show excitement when she and Devin had arrived at the house earlier, but I'd had no energy for pretenses. At least with them, I could be myself, emotional turmoil and all.

"I have no idea what you're talking about."

She snorted, not buying my evasion. Her brown eyes narrowed, and she tilted her head and studied me in the way that made anyone she had on the witness stand think twice before lying to her.

We'd been assigned as roommates when we were barely eighteen and had started law school at Stanford. Our parents thought it would be safest to have us live together. We were both girls from conservative homes whose parents weren't sure what to do with kids who could outthink everyone around them.

Samina's father, an overbearing technology billionaire, had decided for Sam to room with me. He assumed I would be a good influence on his ultra-sheltered daughter, who he wanted to fit into a mold he'd designed. Little had he known that I was just as protected and ready to break free of the confines of family and on the lookout for a partner in crime. From the moment we'd met, we were thick as thieves. The amount of trouble the two of us had gotten into could have given our parents heart attacks. Thankfully, Ashur, Sam's older brother, and Devin, my big bro, kept us from getting into something that would have had dire consequences.

Fifteen years later, we were still getting into mischief together, but our last foray into adventure had gotten us elected as United States senators.

"Okay, then tell me why you barely said a handful of words during lunch and are drinking one of your 'lay an elephant on its ass' drinks at one in the afternoon. I'm the one with a not-yet one-year-old who gets barely any sleep."

"Because I need something to take the edge off." I moved to the sink, rinsed my glass, and then set it in the dish drainer.

"Jaci," Sam said softly. "Did you and Veer break up?"

There was only a small group people who knew about Veer and me. Sam happened to be part of it. Sam had wanted Veer and me together from the time she discovered that I felt more for him than friendship.

Reality was reality. Southern politics was brutal, especially for women, and I was a conservative who couldn't let anything taint my reputation. And a relationship with a liberal outspoken-against-the-GOP real-estate and technology tycoon would tank any chances I had.

Veer knew it, as did I.

We'd resisted the attraction for years, making sure to keep things distant between us. That was, until three years ago. While attending a conference in Las Vegas, I'd run into Veer at my hotel. He had just finished a business meeting with the casino owner, and I was returning to catch a power nap. We'd decided to have dinner, which led to us going out dancing, and then turned into a night of nonstop sex. We had agreed it couldn't go anywhere but kept finding excuses to see each other. Then after returning to Austin, we'd continued to meet up conveniently. Eventually, we'd admitted what we were feeling was more than lust.

"I'm going to take your silence as an affirmative."

I shook my head and turned to face her. "No, I think we're still together."

"Think?" she questioned and then gestured to the seat next to her at the island. "Come here and tell me what's going on. I want to be in the loop. I'm still ticked I learned about Veer and you a year after you guys hooked up. I'm your best friend. You're supposed to tell me shit."

"Whatever," I muttered.

It was only right before our senatorial elections that she'd accidentally discovered Veer and I were more than friends. She happened to have gotten up one morning when she was visiting and caught a half-dressed Veer leaving the house.

The conversation we had after the incident still made me cringe. Samina had made it clear that what we were doing would end up hurting us and, in the end, we'd regret it.

I knew she'd spoken from experience. Sam had accepted being a secret from the world for nearly ten years. She'd married the love of her life only to have both of them pretend nothing was between them and to date other people.

Her high-profile career had been a liability for both

Devin's and my father's careers. In the eyes of the world, Sam was a liberal attorney who took on celebrity clientele. It hadn't mattered that she was well respected or that most of her cases focused on injustices done to her clients. Public knowledge of Devin and Samina's relationship would have made it nearly impossible for Dad to win his reelection bid with his ultra-conservative constituents. Two years ago, right before she announced her candidacy for Senate, she'd decided she'd had enough of living behind the scenes and took the steps to separate from Devin.

It had been the kick in the pants my big brother needed to fix his marriage. Now, Devin and Sam's marriage was stronger than ever, and they had my gorgeous nephew, who was the perfect combination of the two of them.

"I said sit."

"You're so damn bossy," I muttered but followed her instructions by sliding onto the barstool.

I threaded my fingers together, setting them on the island, and stared at my hands, not knowing where to start. After a few minutes, Sam covered my hands with hers, and I sighed. It was time to admit out loud what I knew was the truth.

"For the last few months, every time we're together, it's like we're bracing for it to end. There is so much tension between us. Veer's career has taken off more than anyone could have imagined, and so has mine. I know it has to happen, but I'm not sure I can do it."

"You have to decide what's more important. Your

career or your relationship with Veer. What you want for the future comes with a steep price. You and Veer aren't the only ones affected by your decision. You have to think of Kevin too. As far as the public knows, he's the man in your life."

There was no judgment in her voice. She was one of those people who told me her opinions but would support any decision I made, even if it pissed her off.

She'd known Veer longer than I had. He was her older brother Ashur's best friend. Veer was an only child and had become part of Sam's family, spending any and all free time at Sam's house. Veer was as much Sam's brother as Ashur was. Even with this bond, Sam hadn't taken sides. She was as loyal to me as she was to Veer.

Hell, from the sound of it, she'd taken Kevin into her fold as well.

My lips trembled. "Why did I let things go past that weekend in Vegas?"

"Because both of you have had the hots for each other since we were in law school. I'm surprised you guys waited as long as you did to jump each other's bones."

I couldn't deny her observation. From the moment we'd first met, Veer and I shared an unspoken chemistry that was hard to ignore.

"I knew better. Hell, we both did. And still, we went down this rabbit hole. Any advice on how not to have my heart bleed out when the inevitable happens?"

"Besides what I've already said, I don't have anything. If you recall, I'm the idiot who allowed my husband to keep me a secret for years. If I recall, you were the resident sage who advised me to leave your brother and take him for all he had."

"Thank God the two of you got it together and figured your shit out. For the record, I would have gone with you in the divorce." I gave her a mischievous grin. "No brother was going to get in the way of our sisterhood."

"I second both your statements."

The grandfather clock in the hallway leading out of the kitchen chimed.

"Let's table this for now. Everyone will arrive soon, and I want this weekend to be fun."

"I'm right there with you. I don't think I could take another filibuster attempt like we had this past week," Sam said. "Sometimes I ask myself why the hell I wanted to become a politician when all we do is listen to endless discussions that lead nowhere."

"It comes with the territory. Think about it this way— you only have five years left and then can go back to representing shock jocks like Clint Bassett."

Sam winced and then laughed. "Be nice. If it weren't for him, that asshole Decker would never have been outed for all the crap he did to us."

I pushed down the anger that surfaced whenever anyone mentioned Grey Decker Senior. I shouldn't let the man affect me so much, but sometimes I couldn't help it. He'd helped his son cover up his assault on me and then tried to make it look like I was a drunk whore.

The sad part was Decker would never get over his

hatred of me, especially since I'd come out on top and ousted him from office. He'd probably be a thorn in my side until the day he died, obsessing with tactics to ruin my reputation.

"Jacinta." Sam touched my arm. "I didn't mean to bring up Decker."

"It's okay, Sam. It's not like how it used to be. Even if the memories are still there, neither of the Deckers have power over me anymore."

"That's true. Senior and Junior are lucky if anyone takes them seriously after what came out in the election."

Two years ago, Grey Decker Senior had hired a reporter to take compromising pictures of Sam. Decker thought to use the images to destroy Sam's credibility, thinking that, since she was my sister-in-law and my best friend, hurting her would trickle down to me.

Too bad for Decker that Clint Bassett had exposed him for the douchebag he was. He'd released a recording where Decker discussed selling the pictures for the right price. Clint was the father of four daughters and took the possible attack on Sam as a personal insult to a woman he'd decided was as much a daughter to him as she was his attorney.

Samina had turned the horrible situation to her advantage, using the platform of getting rid of the establishment and anyone who'd support the destruction of people for political gain.

"Sometimes I wish I'd been strong like you and come out about what the Deckers did to me."

"What happened to me and what you experienced are two different things. Decker Junior assaulted you and tried to make it look like you wanted it. Plus, there were other factors, so don't belittle what you went through."

"I know." I sighed.

Both my father and Tyler had been up for election, and any scandal would have ruined their chances to win. No matter how the world viewed things, any hint of impropriety would have destroyed their campaigns and so I kept quiet. Thankfully, my beautiful best friend had used her family's connections to get any inkling of the incident erased so that no one could hurt me again.

"I wished I'd thought of doing more than just wiping their servers."

"I'm glad all you did was use your tech peeps to break into the Decker estate. Neither of us would look good in yellow stripes."

"Whatever, you never let me have any fun."

"Sam," I said in a low voice, "thank you for always being there for me."

She leaned her head against my shoulder. "We're sisters from different misters and all that." She sniffed. "Dammit, you're making me all sappy. Go fix another drink or something." She waved her hand.

A beep sounded, and my head of security, CJ, spoke over the intercom.

"Ms. Camden, Ms. Zain's car left the airport thirty minutes ago, and she will arrive in the next fifteen minutes."

"Thanks for the update," I called out and then stood.

"Come on. Since you ordered me to do it, you can help me. Let's get some refreshments ready. I know Tara will need a pick-me-up after her sixteen-hour flight."

"Can you believe it, the three of us under the same roof again. Lord help the guys." Sam dabbed at her eyes and laughed.

All of a sudden, an uneasy look crossed Sam's face, and she got up from her spot and opened the drink refrigerator, pulling out sparkling water and pouring herself a glass of the fizzy liquid.

I moved to the bar storage and began pulling out bottles of my favorite liquor.

"Want me to add a splash of vodka and pomegranate liquor into that?" Vodka-pomegranate was Sam's go-to drink.

She shook her head. "Nope. I'm good."

I watched her rub her stomach as if to calm it.

Hmmm, Sam never turned down her favorite drink, and her emotions were all over the place. Hadn't she been about to fall into a ball of tears a second ago? Something was up. Then it came to me. The little witch was keeping secrets.

"Sam?"

"Yes."

"How far along are you?"

Surprise crossed her face and then a smile appeared. "Eleven weeks."

"Eleven weeks? Why am I only learning this now?"

"Because it was a secret. Promise not to say anything to anyone. Dev wants to tell the family next month when everyone comes up for Dru's first birthday."

I made the motion of an X over my heart and stuck out my little finger, which I clasped with hers. "I cross my heart and pinky promise."

At that moment, Devin walked in. "Should I be worried? It's never good when you two swear each other to secrecy."

"You'll have to wait and see." Sam lifted a brow.

Sam's face lit up as Devin approached her, turning her chair toward him.

"As long as I don't have to keep you from being arrested, I'm good." He tucked her hair behind her ear and kissed her forehead. "One time was more than enough."

My heart clenched. The love between them was visible to anyone who saw them together.

At least my best friend would get her happily ever after.

I shook the sadness from my mind. No time to wallow —it was time to enjoy my weekend. Who knew how long it would be before I had another free one?

I jumped into gear and started the prep for our snacks.

CHAPTER FIVE

"Tara. I can't believe you're finally here," I shouted as I rushed down the front steps of the house and wrapped my arms around my dear friend Tara Zain.

"I need this so much, Jaci. Thank you for inviting me." Tara squeezed me tight.

As one of the top attorneys in the United States who specialized in international law and human rights, she epitomized a badassed, take-no-one's-shit negotiator. She had been dubbed "The Commander" by those she'd faced while handling various cases around the world.

In the past few weeks, she'd gotten more than her fair share of media coverage after she negotiated the nonviolent release of a group of kidnapped girls whose captors planned to sell as child brides in a remote region between India and Pakistan. There had been a lot of controversy and criticism about her role, especially since our government hadn't sanctioned her involvement.

President Edgar's disinterest in the situation had frustrated me to no end, especially since there were at least seventy American children involved. When Tara stepped in and invited the media, she'd put a spotlight on the lack of action by the current administration in matters of international affairs. In the end, people viewed Tara as a hero but at the cost of her privacy.

Neither the president nor Tara knew I had a plan up my sleeve if things didn't calm down by the end of the coming week. It was risky and could potentially cause me severe backlash, but it was worth it to do the right thing while protecting my friend.

I knew for a fact if Tara had been a man and aligned with the Republican Party, President Edgar would have jumped at the chance to celebrate the successful release of the children. Hell, the only reason the chauvinistic ass praised me at every opportunity was to make himself look less bigoted and more open minded.

If he only realized that half our party couldn't stand him and could see right through his words to the man underneath.

"You have no idea how long I've waited for this weekend to get here," I told Tara.

"Are you sure having me under your roof won't politically hurt you?"

I guided her toward the house. "You need us, and I will never turn my back on you."

"I've missed you and Samina so much. It's been nearly two years since we've done anything together." She gave me a weary but genuine smile. "Mom and Dad told me you need to come to the house next time you're in Seattle."

"I wouldn't miss seeing them for the world. Your mom's cooking is to die for. I've always wondered how you kept your hot body when you grew up eating her food."

"It wasn't easy, but soccer and track helped keep my metabolism charged." She adjusted the straps of her bag and scanned the yard. "Who's going to be here?"

The tension in her shoulders told me she wanted to know about one specific person.

"Don't worry. Sam said Ashur had a meeting in New York, so he couldn't make it."

She visibly relaxed.

Tara and Ashur had been a couple the summer before Tara had left for college. Ashur had just graduated from Harvard and was transitioning into his role in his father's company when he'd run into Tara, who was interning on the data collections floor.

They'd fallen for each other so hard, but Ashur's father had orchestrated the demise of the relationship. He was against his son having any relationship with the daughter of a no-name programmer in his company. Minesh Kumar expected his children to marry within their circle of influence, and Tara was definitely not part of that group. Ashur's father threatened Tara into choosing between Ashur and her family's livelihood. In the end, Tara called it off with Ashur. She'd never told him the reason, and until a few years ago she hadn't known that Minesh Kumar had told his son that she'd left him for another man.

"Good. I'm not ready for any incident with Ashur. He hasn't gotten over the past, and I'm too tired right now to battle with him or his representatives."

I frowned. "Did I miss something? When did you guys interact? Last I knew, the two of you avoided each other like the plague."

During Samina's election, Tara had used honed disinterest to handle any contact involving Ashur, pretending she couldn't see him or his six-foot-three frame.

"Do me a favor, forget I said anything. I need a relaxing weekend without any reminders of the world outside your gates."

"Okay, I hear you. Let's partake in a few drinks and lounge by the pool before dinner. I have all your favorite food on the menu."

"That sounds incredible. Hopefully, I'll be able to roll out of here by the end of the weekend."

"GOD, THIS IS THE LIFE," TARA SAID AS SHE RELAXED back in her lounge chair.

She wore dark gold-rimmed shades that matched the beading on her bikini, giving her the look of a world-traveling goddess. The golden hue of her skin made me envious and wish I could tan as beautifully as she could without burning.

"No kidding. Now the only thing missing is a hot

cabana boy to wait on us," I said and then sipped my cocktail.

Thoughts of Veer wearing a tight pair of board shorts and serving me drinks popped into my mind. That would be the perfect addition to the day.

"Stop thinking of my almost-brother as if he were some edible candy. That's gross." Samina came to sit at the bottom of my deck chair and handed me a bottle of sunscreen. "Put this on before you burn. You, my dear, aren't blessed with the golden complexions Tara and I are."

Sam's soft pink-and-blue long-sleeved chiffon cover-up showed the slight swell of her pregnant belly underneath. No one would know her little secret unless they were looking. She was so beautiful. I'd told her pregnancy made her glow and it was true.

"Yes, ma'am." I took the container, squeezed out a quarter-sized amount, and began to rub the protective lotion onto my arms and legs. "Fantasizing about the man I'm with is a huge difference from you banging my brother every chance you get and not hiding the fact. At least Veer and I keep it under the radar."

"What? Wait." Tara coughed and sat up, taking off her glasses. "I thought you were seeing Kevin. Did you guys break up? Someone tell me when you and Veer George started bumping uglies? I've been out of the country, but I would have heard any gossip about the governor of Texas and the junior senator from Texas."

"Yeah, about that. You see. We umm..." It had been so long since Tara and I had gotten together that she'd never learned about the change in Veer's and my relationship status.

"The reason you haven't heard about it—" Sam pushed my legs to the side and then shimmied her body into the minuscule space next to me, "—is because the two dummies have it under wraps. Kevin is the cover for their illicit affair."

"Sam, there are at least four other loungers for you to use. We don't have to share one as if we were little kids who can't be without each other."

"You're comfy." She rested her head on her hand and leaned against my thighs.

I rolled my eyes. "Veer and I weren't supposed to happen."

"I knew you'd end up jumping each other one day. There was always this undercurrent of sexual tension with you two." Tara set her glasses back on her face and then took a sip of her drink.

I frowned. Was everyone around me aware that we'd had the hots for each other for years? I guessed so if Tara picked up on it.

"Anyway," I interjected, "now that we're together, we have to protect our careers."

Tara nodded. "I get it. If you want the Republican nomination in four years, you can't be seen as a liberal. And coming out with Veer as your man will cost you dearly, no matter your conservative voting record."

I stared at her. She'd hit the nail on the head with minimal information.

"Don't look at me like that. Why do you think I haven't gotten into anything serious with any of the guys I've dated over the last few years? I'm a human rights attorney with many liberal ties. Any man who gets involved with me will have to be someone who can handle my agenda and my ability to get into politically costly situations."

"Or maybe it has to do with the fact you're still in love with my brother," Sam said, not looking in Tara's direction, but smiling like the Cheshire cat. "For the record, he's not over you, either."

"Sam, I know you mean well, but you have to stop meddling. Ashur and I are ancient history. I gave up that dream years ago." Tara clenched her jaw and gazed out into the distance. "All I can hope for is that we can be in the same room without it filling with tension. So far, we're failing miserably."

Something besides the media fallout from the last week was happening.

"What's going on, Tara?" I asked and looked at Sam, who shrugged her shoulders. "We're here for you. Did you and Ashur hook up and it went badly?"

Tara set her cocktail down. "God no, nothing like that."

"Then what?" Sam probed.

"I suggest you ask Veer. He knows all about it." Tara released a deep sigh. "Can we please forget about everything else and veg? The next few days are going to be my only free weekend for months. You see, my law partner decided to become a senator and left me with ten years' worth of cases."

"Sorry, not sorry," Sam retorted. "I have enough on my plate with members of the Senate."

"On second thought, I'd rather deal with the Clint Bassetts of the world than deal with members of Congress. I say, more power to the both of you." Tara lifted her glass toward Sam and me with a grin, then almost immediately her smile disappeared. She slipped to sitting, and her relaxed demeanor turned tense.

I glanced in the direction she looked and nearly swallowed my tongue.

Veer, Ashur, and Kevin walked in our direction.

Damn, they looked good. The three men oozed masculine power and confidence. They were all well over six feet tall with bodies honed from years in the military and triathlon training. The first time I'd seen them together, I'd thought a girl had to be dead not to notice their sex appeal. They'd just returned from a tour in Afghanistan and had come down to New Orleans for Mardi Gras. By the end of the long weekend, they'd had every woman they'd encountered thinking unladylike thoughts.

"Nice outfit, Jaci." Veer scanned me from head to toe, making me feel a tingle that I should have assuaged with his body earlier in the morning.

"Thank you." I licked my lips and sat up. The last thing I wanted anyone to notice was the arousal pooling between my legs. Thankfully my bikini top had enough embroidery to hide my pebbled nipples.

Ashur's expression was anything but happy. He stared

at Tara with an intensity that said he either wanted to fuck her senseless or yell at her. It was probably both. I was going to have to have a long talk with Veer about inviting Ashur when he knew Tara was going to be at the house.

I peeked at Sam, who had a scowl to match her brother's. She glanced my way and mouthed, "What the fuck is he doing here?"

I shrugged and mouthed back, "He's your brother, how should I know?"

"Hello, ladies. Devin asked me to tell you the caterers have just left, and everything is ready for dinner." Kevin approached me, leaning down to kiss my cheek. "Are you planning on feeding an army?"

"One thing you can say is that you never leave my house hungry."

"That's true, I can't dispute that." He moved to greet Sam.

"Hiya, handsome." Sam reached up and hugged Kevin tight and then gestured to Tara. "Kevin, have you met my law partner? Tara Zain, this is the super handsome Kevin Stanton."

Kevin moved toward her and crouched down beside her.

"Hello. I can't express what a privilege it is to meet you in person. I follow all the adventures of Commander Zain." He took Tara's hand in his and kissed it. "Is it true that you told the terrorist Usaf Nazarri to go fuck himself when he refused to negotiate with you because you were a woman?"

"Don't believe everything you hear," Tara said tightly, and I knew those words were directed at the man whose presence she was doing her best to ignore. "Perception and hearsay aren't always reality."

"If I were you, I'd be proud of the press coverage. You've started a movement that has brought attention to the plight of women across the world. You'd make a fabulous running mate for Jacinta in four years." Kevin winked at me.

His idea had merit. Once the drama of Tara's current situation with the president calmed and her name was cleared, hopefully sooner rather than later, if my plan came through, her liberal side would be the perfect companion to my conservatism. Together, we'd appeal to a majority of voters. I'd have to talk about this in private with Tara sometime during this weekend.

Never mind. Strike that thought.

If I couldn't be seen with Veer as the man in my life, having Tara with me on the ticket would be even more detrimental. Her stance on issues was twice as liberal and leftist as Veer's.

"Uh-oh, I see the wheels turning," Kevin said. "I'd be worried, Tara, very worried."

I caught the amused gleam in Kevin's eyes. He knew as well as I did that Tara wasn't even a remote possibility. He was only steering the conversation away from the tension between Ashur and Tara.

Tara smirked. "I'm familiar with her antics. Too bad for her that I won't be old enough when the time comes to pick a running mate. I don't turn thirty-five until after the election."

I huffed and then stood.

"Shot down before the idea could take root. I completely forgot you're a baby compared to us." I walked toward Ashur, hoping if I brought him into the conversation, he'd stop staring daggers into Tara. "How's it going, grumpy?"

He moved his gaze from Tara to me and smirked. "As usual. Nothing new to report."

"Right. I buy that. You're always up to something, Ashur Kumar. How was New York?"

"Uneventful. My meeting never happened because I was stood up." He glanced behind me at Tara for a second. "I guess they had better things to do."

Okay, something was definitely up between those two and it was more than their past. When I got Veer alone, he was going to get an earful.

"Think of it this way—you get to spend a fabulous weekend with three gorgeous women and your closest friends."

A smile touched his lips. "I can see the merits of that."

I threaded my arm through his and turned us toward the house. "Come on, everyone. Let's freshen up and have dinner."

CHAPTER SIX

"They haven't killed each other," I said to Kevin, a little before eight as we walked down the path leading to the gazebo overlooking the Colorado River. "Dinner was fun, albeit a bit tense."

"It's early." Kevin adjusted the drink cooler he carried in his hands. "Besides, they're avoiding one another. I cringe to think what it will be like if they end up alone. At least we have Tyler to play buffer."

At the beginning of dinner, Ashur and Tara had taken opposite ends of the room and for the most part engaged in various conversations around us. It wasn't until my twin Tyler arrived from DC that the mood lightened in the house. Tyler had announced no shop talk was allowed. He'd endured a hellish week in the House like I had in the Senate, and all he wanted to do was pretend he wasn't a grown-up for one weekend.

He'd ordered me to keep drinks and laughter flowing.

And since I lived on a private estate, my security would keep anyone who thought to invade our hiatus from public life at a distance.

All of my security personnel were former Navy Seals who'd gone into private protection. And anyone who thought to cross them would encounter five very angry men who would kick the trespasser's ass.

"Since we're alone, I have a bone to pick with you, Senator Camden."

I had a feeling I was about to get my ass handed to me. I'd made what Veer and I shared a secret. The only thing Kevin knew was that we saw each other on occasion to scratch an itch. Now, with the heated looks Veer and I sent each other, there was no way of hiding the true depths of our feelings.

"Okay. What did I do now?"

"Why didn't you tell me that you and Veer were a hell of a lot more than fuck buddies?"

I opened my mouth to deny it instinctively but shut it fast when Kevin glared at me.

"Don't even pretend that you have no idea what I'm talking about. I saw the looks the two of you were passing. Hell, if it weren't for the ice between Ash and Tara the room would have combusted from the emotions and sexual tension between the two of you."

I cringed and then felt my cheeks heat. Veer had taken every opportunity to brush by me or give me his I-plan-to-fuck-you-stupid looks. There was no way I could hide my reaction to him. For most of dinner, my libido was doing overtime as was my will to keep from jumping Veer right in front of everybody.

"For the same reason you haven't told me who you're dating or that you are head-over-heels in love with him."

"Mine could ruin our careers."

I stopped walking and folded my arms. "Did you forget it would be the same for me?"

"It is night-and-day different to be found out you were dating a liberal than for anyone to find out I'm gay. Yours is about ambition, not your sexuality."

I sighed. "Sorry, there's no contest. I'm an asshole."

"It's okay, Jaci." Kevin set the cooler on the ground and then wrapped an arm around my waist. "Did you think I wouldn't approve?"

"Well, since Veer is one of your closest friends, I thought you'd be pissed when you found out that our relationship had gotten deeper than scratching an itch. After all, you and I are the ones positioning ourselves to get married."

"Do you think I would ever begrudge you happiness?" He turned me to face him. "Just as you'd do for me, I would step aside without a thought. Besides, I'd hoped it would become more than the two of you scratching an itch."

"For the record, I was the one who convinced Veer to keep the depth of our relationship under wraps."

He lifted a brow. "I have no doubt it was all your idea. Veer isn't a sneaking-around kind of guy. He's more in your face. If he did this, he's in love with you."

"And I love him."

"Baby girl. You've been in love with him for the past ten years. I'm just glad you finally did something about it, instead of pining for him from afar."

I frowned. "How would you know this?"

"I'm not blind. I knew how you felt since Veer and Ashur deployed for the first time. Then when Veer and Ash were shot down, you took it as hard as Samina did."

I hated thinking about the day I'd learned the news. I'd come back to the apartment I'd shared to find Sam rolled into a ball on our couch crying. No matter what I'd done, I couldn't get her to tell me what happened. After a little while, I'd pieced together some of the puzzle and called my father, who could get details. He'd used his connections to learn Veer and Ashur had gone missing a week earlier. Insurgents had held them captive until a rescue mission found them barely conscious and with severe injuries. The base doctors had placed them in medically induced comas to keep them stable and then transferred them to Germany for further treatment.

Thankfully, Kevin was working on a different assignment that kept him restricted to the base. When I'd emailed him for information on the status of Veer and Ashur, he'd told me it was classified, and he wasn't allowed to give me any updates.

For weeks, both Sam and I were walking zombies, going to class, work, and then back home to study. We'd shut ourselves in our apartment. The only visitor we had was Devin. He'd come to see Sam every chance he'd gotten to keep her strong. My poor brother had had no clue that I needed comfort too.

"You're right. Veer meant something to me from the first time I met him." I took a seat on the cooler and Kevin joined me.

"If it makes you feel better—" he nudged my elbow, "—he had the hots for you back then too."

I scrunched my face. "Right, I buy that."

"You learn a lot about a man when you're stuck in a foreign country for months on end. He had it bad for you, but he knew as well as you did that you ran in different circles that could never mix. He was a liberal even then, and we were in the middle of combat."

"Apparently it didn't stop us in the long run."

"It was bound to happen. And Vegas provided the perfect opportunity to act on your attraction."

"How did you figure out it was Vegas?"

I'd never told Kevin when my affair with Veer had started. I'd only said to him that Veer and I hooked up whenever I was in town.

He scoffed. "You may be the child prodigy, but it doesn't take a rocket scientist to look back and see when the vibe between the two of you changed from innocent flirtation to a constant emission of lust."

"Hey, it's all your fault. If you hadn't left me at your swank hotel to go do grown-up stuff in your family's oil biz, I wouldn't have drunk too much and ended up in this predicament."

Kevin snorted. "You two would have ended up

jumping each other sooner or later. Sam and I had a bet when it would happen. We'd only hoped it wouldn't be while you were with other people."

"I am with someone else—you," I pointed out.

"We aren't the same thing, and you know it."

"I know." A wave of sadness flooded down on me. "Kev, what are we going to do?"

"I don't have much choice in the matter. I was willing to come out, but I couldn't be the only one risking everything. You, on the other hand, will lose the nomination but gain the man you love."

"How do I give up everything I've worked for since I was a child? It's within my grasp. I have to wait four more years, and I know I'll become the first female to win the White House."

"He's more than worth risking it. I've gone to combat with him. I've never known a man who does the right thing even when it costs him like Veer George. He's perfect for you. Well, with the exception of his liberal-leaning tendencies."

"There is that one negative." I couldn't help but laugh. However, the amusement died quickly. "I feel like no matter what I do I'm fucked."

"True, true. But there is only one choice where you'll get fucked on the regular and like it."

I shook my head. "You are so wrong."

"Hey just telling you how I see it."

"Come on, before they send out a search party." I stood and brushed my summer dress down.

Kevin rose and turned toward the cooler. "It would be for the alcohol, not us."

At that moment, Tyler's shout came from the area along the river. "Jaci, you promised to keep the drinks flowing. You're failing miserably."

Kevin picked up the cooler. "It's a wonder you didn't strangle him in vitro. I have no idea how he keeps the world from seeing this goofball instead of the staunch Southern member of the United States House of Representatives."

"We all have our facades." I saw Veer come toward us. "Why don't you head down? I want to talk to V." I said that loudly enough for Veer to hear me.

Kevin nodded to Veer as he passed him and murmured, "Glad it's you in trouble and not me."

As Veer approached, my heartbeat accelerated, and a flood of desire pooled between my legs. He'd changed into casual khaki shorts and a light blue cotton button-down that accentuated the muscular build of his arms. Lust filled his gaze, and the thought of taking him back to the house and having my wicked way with him had my body heating.

"Stop staring at me like that or I'm taking you inside to make good on the dirty thoughts running through your mind."

"I don't see a problem with your idea." I set my fingers on his shoulder and stood on tiptoes.

"Are you sure you want to miss the s'mores?" He gave me a sly grin. "Tyler has a bag of giant marshmallows and three bars of Ghirardelli dark chocolate waiting for you."

My weakness was the ooey gooey goodness of melted chocolate and marshmallows sandwiched between graham crackers. I could eat them for breakfast, lunch, and dinner. Thankfully, I had a willpower of iron otherwise I wouldn't be able to fit through a door.

"That's mean. How can I choose?"

He slipped his hands around my waist and pulled me against him. He grazed his stubble against my jaw.

"It's easy. What do you want more, sex or chocolate?"

"Can I have both?" I asked, a bit too breathless.

Before he could respond, I heard Samina shout, "Get a room. There are innocent eyes here."

Both Veer and I laughed and then I said, "She's one to talk with the number of times I've caught Dev and her in the middle of something. At least we aren't groping each other."

It felt so good not to hide what Veer and I had. On this estate, we were safe. I wasn't the Republican senator, and Veer wasn't the governor. We were a couple. Well, at least for this weekend.

I stepped out of his hold and offered him my hand. "Come with me."

He slid his palm over mine, and we walked toward the pool house. No one would disturb us there.

"Want to tell me why I'm in trouble? It can't be our activities of the morning. If I recall, you came three times."

I licked my lips, and a quiver shot into my core.

"No, it's not about your sexual prowess."

"Then what?" He opened the gate leading to the walkway.

"Why did you invite Ashur when I specifically told you that Tara was coming down? This weekend was supposed be stress free for Tara. She's tense and no way near relaxed. After the way President Edgar turned her efforts into something to investigate, she needs a break."

"Jaci, there are things in play that make it necessary for Tara and Ashur to get over their issues. Their future rides on it."

I gave Veer the side eye. "Care to explain that statement?"

"Nope. It's between them. Come on." Veer wrapped his arm around the back of my waist and opened the front door leading to a small living room.

I stopped walking, slipping out of his hold. "If it is between them, then why are you involved?"

"Jaci, let it go." He stared with his "I am boss, you are little woman" glare.

I cocked a hand on my hip. "Would you let it go if I were keeping something from you?"

"Aren't you?" He folded his arms, continuing to hold my annoyed gaze.

"What the fuck does that mean?"

"Aren't you just waiting for the right time to announce your engagement to Kevin?"

"Nothing is set. You should know as well as I do that the press likes to sensationalize things."

"He is your significant other, for all purposes." The

bitterness in his voice made my heart ache.

"No, he is not," I countered. "We're friends. Nothing more. You're the man I want."

"Does he know this? I know when a man is in love with you. I see it every time I look in the mirror. So, cut the bullshit."

"For the love of God, Veer. I'm a sister to him. Our relationship is about politics and inheritances, not romance."

"Maybe you see it that way, but he may not."

"You are the one who suggested Kevin and I pretend to be a couple. So, if anyone is to blame for this predicament, it's you. And just for the record, he's in a relationship with someone else."

"Who?"

"I can't tell you."

"Fine. Keep your secrets, and I'll keep mine." He moved past me to a bar cart stationed next to the kitchen island.

He poured himself a finger of cognac and shot it back. "Do you love him?"

"You're kidding, right?"

"Just answer the question."

I shook my head at him like he was an idiot. "Of course I do."

"I see." A look of devastation passed across Veer's face.

With a sigh, I approached him, taking the glass and setting it on the cart. I cupped his face in my hand and rested my forehead against his.

"No, you don't. I love Kevin the way I love Devin, Tyler, and Ashur. Like a brother."

He pulled back, blowing out a breath of relief. The hurt in his eyes softened but still lingered.

"Jaci. This is tearing us apart. I want to strangle Kevin for having the part of you that I'll never get."

Guilt sat heavy in my stomach. I was doing this. Veer was the most confident man I'd ever known, and now I was making him doubt how I felt about him. I knew I should do the unselfish thing and tell him we should end this right now. But I couldn't do it. Breaking up would mean I'd lose my happily ever after. Who was I kidding? I never had it.

"I'm sorry. I..." He placed a finger to my lips, cutting off my words.

"I know." He kissed my forehead. "I know."

He lifted me, bunching my dress up and wrapping my legs around his waist, and sealed our mouths together. Desire ignited throughout my body, heating me from the inside out. We devoured each other, our tongues dueling and playing.

Veer nipped my lower lip as he set me on the island.

"Veer." I gazed into his eyes.

"Yes." He pushed me back onto the granite and cupped my breasts in his hands, pinching and rolling the puckered tips.

My core contracted, and a gush of wetness soaked my cleft. I arched into Veer's delicious touch, and my legs tightened around his waist.

"I want sex."

He laughed. "Isn't that what we are doing?"

"No." I lifted my head to look him in the eyes. "I mean I want you to fuck me. Hard, dirty. No foreplay."

He paused his kneading of my swollen mounds. "Why?"

"Because I want to feel the delicious sting with each step I take tonight. I want my pussy sore, knowing you'd fucked me so hard with your thick cock that I ached."

A devilish light entered his eyes, completely replacing the sadness from a moment earlier.

I loved when he was gentle, the lover who put my needs always before his. But there was something about it when it was raw and rough.

"You want to be fucked, Jaci." He shifted and moved his hand to the front of his pants, unbuttoning and then lowering his zipper. "I'll fuck you."

His cock sprang free of its confines and bobbed between us. A drop of pre-cum dripped from the tip, making me lick my lips. I wanted a taste of his delicious essence. I'd craved it last night, and I craved it now.

"Eyes up here. You wanted me to fuck you, and that's what we're going to do. You can suck my cock at another time."

He reached under my dress and ripped my underwear and in the next second, he thrust balls-deep.

I cried out from the pleasure-pain of his girth pushing through my swollen, slick cleft. I arched up and gripped Veer's forearms.

"Yes," I cried out. "Hard. Please give it to me hard."

He pounded my throbbing pussy, setting a pace that only allowed me to hold on. The teeth of his zipper pressed into my butt cheeks with each stroke. I couldn't help but enjoy the harsh feel of the metal against my tender skin.

I wanted him to imprint himself into me, to make everything disappear but us.

He gripped my hip as the finger of his other hand came around my throat in a firm but gentle hold. He gave a slight squeeze, and my core spasmed around his pummeling cock. He repeated the action, and my mind clouded. This man owned me in a way no one else ever would. My need grew to a point I couldn't hold out any longer. My core trembled, clutching desperately around his thick cock.

"Veeer," I stuttered. "I need..."

"Come now," he ordered.

My body responded, contracting and pulsing, shaking violently. Veer released a guttural groan as his cock began to swell. He was tight and full, on the verge of his own orgasm. His neck arched and his jaw clenched. He threw his head back and came with a loud cry.

Veer dropped his head to my chest, both of us breathing in short pants. I kept my legs wrapped around his waist and sighed.

The door to the house opened, making us stiffen.

"Jaci, where the fuck are you? Sam told me to..." Devin walked in with Ashur and came to an abrupt stop. "Oh, for the love of God. Man, that's my baby sister." Devin covered his eyes.

"Payback's a bitch, isn't it?" Ashur said.

CHAPTER SEVEN

An hour after Devin and Ashur caught Veer and me at the tail end of our mutual climaxes, I leaned against the back wall of the estate's giant family room.

Devin scowled as he glanced my way, and I smirked in response, lifting my cocktail glass in his direction.

"What are you smiling at?" Veer asked me as he came to stand next to me.

"My brother and the horror he keeps reliving every time he looks at either of us."

"As Ashur said, payback's a bitch. I've lost count of the number of times one of us has disturbed or walked in on his sexual antics with Samina. After over ten years of their shit, Devin deserved what he got."

I shook my head and offered Veer a taste of my drink. "True, but it's still weird to have my big brother find me orgasming while one of his closest friends was fucking my brains out."

"He'll get over it." Veer set a hand on my waist and took a sip of the drink, wincing at the potent taste of the concoction Tyler had created for me. "Damn, that's strong. It's almost as bad as your drinks. Except Tyler's have something other than alcohol in them."

"Very funny, smartass." I smiled up at him.

Veer's phone beeped, causing him to pull it out of his pocket. When he scanned the incoming message, he frowned and released a groan.

"What's wrong?"

"Nothing really, just Abigail reminding me I have to review the changes to the state budget I'm going to propose on Monday."

I smirked. "You know the state Senate and House are going to hand you your ass for the comments you made about our president's budget?"

"I've already accounted for the possibility."

"Of course you have." I rubbed the frown line forming between his brows. "If you want, I can review it and give you a Republican perspective?"

He studied me for a few seconds and then gestured to the people in the room. "Wouldn't that take you away from the festivities here?"

"Tyler can take over." I glanced at my twin, who was going into a lively description of a situation he'd gotten into with a fellow House member. "Besides, how many times have you helped me figure out all the holes in my plans? Let me return the favor."

Veer kissed the top of my head, stepped back, and then offered me his elbow. "Thank you. Let me hear your conservative point of view, so I can figure out a way to battle your ass-backwards party members."

"You think you're so funny." I laughed and tucked my arm into his.

———————————

A LITTLE BEFORE SEVEN IN THE MORNING, I CREPT out of my room, making sure not to wake Veer. After spending a few hours reviewing Veer's budget and debating all the obstacles he would face, we'd spent most of the night making love. I should have been exhausted, but I couldn't sleep.

Today would be a day of relaxation. The guys planned to go out to Lake Travis for some fishing and we ladies would go for a visit to a fashion designer friend of mine who had a private showroom and then return to the house for more poolside vegging. We would all meet back for dinner, where Tyler would wow us with his grill master skills. My twin was a killer chef when it came to an open flame, and I said more power to him.

Right as I approached the back steps leading to the kitchen, I ran into the very brother I was thinking about. He was covered in sweat and wearing a soaked T-shirt and shorts.

"Good morning. Why are you up so early?"

Tyler ran a hand through his damp blond hair. "Ashur and I went for a run on the property. We're both training for the Boston Marathon."

"Shit. I forgot you qualified." I winced. "Can you forgive me for not congratulating you?"

Last month, Tyler had run the Houston Marathon with Ashur. They were running fanatics and had decided they wanted to qualify for the mother of all races, the Boston Marathon.

"Sure, if you give me a hug this minute." He lifted his wet arm. "Fair is fair."

I ducked under him. "You keep that stinky boy smell away from me. Plus, the race isn't until next year. Why are you training now?"

He gave me an annoyed glare. "I have to run every fucking day if I don't want to die when the race actually happens."

"Sorry. I'm not the runner, I don't know how this works. I'm a Pilates and yoga girl."

"Weak," he said as he moved toward his bedroom.

"Excuse me? Stop right there," I ordered. "Want to repeat that? Who's the one who complained that he pulled a groin muscle the last time he challenged me to a session of Tabata on the reformer?"

He ran a hand across his sweaty face. "Don't remind me. I could barely sit for a week."

"I rest my case."

"Whatever, go play good host and make me breakfast. I am a guest, after all."

I snorted and took the steps down to the kitchen.

Guest, my ass. He was part owner of this estate. I wasn't my fault he lived in Louisiana most of the time.

As I stepped onto the lower landing, I came to an abrupt stop. A loud, heated conversation was ensuing between Ashur and Tara. I peeked around the corner to see Tara's hands braced on the granite of the island and Ashur standing with his arms folded across his chest in the posture I'd dubbed "the wall." He was on a mission to get answers, and he wasn't going to let Tara go until he got them.

I'd hoped they'd continue ignoring each other so the weekend wouldn't have any more tension, but I guessed it was too much to ask. I knew there was a lot more to what had broken Ashur and Tara up than Sam and Ashur's father orchestrating the demise of the relationship. Whatever it was, neither one of them had gotten over it.

"What do you want from me?"

"I want the truth."

"You wouldn't believe me even if I told you the truth."

"Try me."

"Ashu, please. Leave me alone."

"Don't call me that. You don't ever get to call me that again. The nickname is for my lover, and you're not her. The fact that I popped your cherry means nothing."

Tara flinched, and her shoulders sagged as her grip on the counter intensified.

"Why would you get Veer to contact me if you can't

stand the sight of me?" Tara asked as she focused on something outside the windows.

Ashur leaned his hip against the counter behind Tara, staring at the back of her head. "Because you owe me."

"I owe you shit." Tara's voice quivered.

Ashur clenched his fists. "What about the rich lover whose family pulled strings to get you into Harvard?"

"What the fuck are you talking about? I earned my place there, just like you did. I was fucking valedictorian."

"Answer me something, Commander Zain. Did you sleep with your mystery man as payment that first night in Boston or did you wait a whole week out of respect for our relationship?"

Okay, this had gone on long enough. Whatever happened in their past, I couldn't let Ashur treat Tara like this. She was one of the best people I had ever known.

"I don't have to defend myself to you. You think everyone is like you. The majority of the world wasn't blessed to have parents who could buy their way into things. You should talk to your father about what actually happened instead of making accusations without facts." She took a deep breath and turned, ready to storm out of the room. But she came to an abrupt stop when she saw me.

Her face changed from sadness to emotionless calm. She had it down better than I did. Locking up our feelings was the best way to survive the careers we'd both chosen.

"Ash, leave her alone," I said. "I could hear you up the stairs."

"Stay out of this, Jacinta." He stared at Tara, who held his gaze. "I'm going to get my answers one way or the other. I have too much riding on this."

"You have no idea what I've had to go through or the sacrifices I've had to make to reach the position I have. You can pretend to be the victim of my manipulative plans all you want, but you know the truth, and you refuse to admit you got it wrong.

"What could I have expected? You're just like the man you try so hard not to be like, wanting to use me as a way to achieve your goals. Well, I won't have it. I'll never let another Kumar destroy me again. And believe me, if I agreed to your proposal, you would destroy the little part of me that survived your father."

"So, the answer is no?" Ashur's voice was cold.

"My answer is hell no. You're a bastard, Ashur Kumar. I can't believe I ever thought I loved you." Tara turned and walked out the door with her head held high.

I waited for the sound of footsteps to quiet and I was sure Tara was at a distance away before turning to Ashur.

"I never thought you'd be the asshole you like the world to believe you are. Tara didn't deserve what you just said."

"What do you know about it, Jacinta? I'm not the one juggling two men who love you. When you get your relationships in order, I'll listen to you. God, I hope you aren't sleeping with both of them."

I narrowed my eyes but kept my cool.

"I love you as my own brother, Ashur. And I get you

are hurting, but don't ever take your anger out on me. Whatever happened between the two of you is history, you need to leave it there. Tara is a good person who does the right thing even when it costs her dearly. She isn't the whore you accused her of being."

"I don't know what to believe. Why would my father do this?"

"That man wants to control every aspect of his children's lives. He lost his hold on Samina when she chose Devin over her inheritance. You were the only one he could still manipulate."

"No, he is a lot of things but he wouldn't do that to me. He would never ruin a woman's reputation like that."

"Are you fucking kidding me?" I cocked a hand on my hip. "You know it as well as I do that Minesh Kumar would lie and alter facts to make a situation look the way he wanted. If you hadn't intervened last year, don't you think he would have used his connections to make Samina lose the election? Your father is the type of man who would help Decker in his campaign against Samina if it meant he would win his battle against his own children."

Ashur remained quiet for a few minutes, digesting my words. He closed his eyes and lifted his face to the sky.

My heart ached for him. With the exception of Tara, Ash was the type of man who always wanted to give people the benefit of the doubt, even when all evidence said he shouldn't. For years, Samina had been the same way. It had taken her father kicking her out of the house to make her see what a bastard the man who had raised her was. Now, Ashur was faced with accepting the truth of his father's nature and the mistakes he'd made with Tara.

"God, I hate that man. All his money and polish, and he destroyed my one chance at happiness." He sighed and shook his head. "I'm sorry, Jacinta. I didn't think seeing her would bring back so many painful feelings. She's more beautiful now than she ever was."

I opened my liquor cabinet, poured two fingers of scotch and handed the glass to Ashur. Yes, it was the ass crack of dawn, but this was a heated situation.

"You're still in love with her."

He threw back the alcohol and set the tumbler on the island. "I don't know."

"Liar."

He snorted. "Maybe."

"I say more than maybe."

He remained quiet for a few seconds, staring at the open door, and then said, "Do me a favor."

"What?" I folded my arms and stared at him. "I'm not kicking Tara out of my house."

"Go check on her." He ran a frustrated hand through his hair. "I...she was right. I'm a bastard. She didn't..." He paused and blew out a deep breath. "Go make sure she's okay."

"Ash, you're a good guy, no matter what you want people to believe."

"Keep that information between us. I have a reputation to uphold."

I nodded and left the room to find Tara.

As I passed the library, I heard the distinct sound of sniffles. I paused and quietly opened the door. Tara stared toward the river through the open balcony doors. Tears gleamed in her eyes, but there was also a hard edge to her face.

It was unusual to see the woman known as the Commander in her international work as anything but poised and always in control of her emotions. Ashur shouldn't have made it sound like she used him to land a bigger fish. He was hurting, and Tara was the collateral damage.

"Tara. Are you okay?" I walked up and took a seat beside her.

She shook her head. "I've faced the worst of humanity and negotiated against the most hardened of criminals without flinching or letting their opinions or actions wound me. And here I am, letting a few choice words from someone who I left years ago make me feel like I'm a selfish, self-centered whore."

"Ashur is a hard man. He had to be, with a father like his. But he's a good guy."

"It doesn't excuse his behavior."

"You're right. But there is a lot of history you have no clue about."

"Believe me, I know. I'm part of it."

I wasn't sure how to respond. The wounds both Tara and Ashur nursed still festered, and I was the last person to give advice. My love life was a mess of its own.

"Maybe coming down this weekend was a bad idea. I should have expected Ashur to make an appearance. Especially after I stood him up in New York. I didn't have the stamina to handle any meetings after the fallout from the No Bride project."

Well hell, I was a dumbass. I should have suspected that Tara was the one who missed the meeting with Ashur. The tension between them was wrapped in way more than past hurts.

"I'd hoped that after all these years if we ever met again..." she paused, "...we could move past what happened when we were kids. I guess I was completely wrong. Seeing him hurts so much, Jaci. I'm thirty years old and haven't gotten over the pain of something that happened when I was eighteen."

"I'm glad you're here. Sam and I missed you. Plus, you needed the break before you collapsed from saving the world."

"What good are all my efforts if people constantly remind me of how I fucked up?"

"If it makes you feel better, you're the only person I've ever seen who ruffles Ashur's feathers, and I've known him for almost fifteen years."

Ashur was hard and ruthless when it came to his business dealings. He kept his emotions under a close-fitting grip, which made him seem like a cold, calculating bastard. He used this persona to his advantage, letting others make their opinions of him.

She gave a tight smile and continued to gaze at the river.

"He never came after me, Jaci. He believed the crap his father told him. He should have known I was lying when I said that I'd never loved him. He never questioned why one minute I was head over heels for him and the next I was walking out the door. What was I supposed to do? I either left Ashur or let Minesh Kumar destroy my family. He's a billionaire. My parents are simple middle-class people who couldn't afford to lose their careers."

"I don't have any words of wisdom. My life is pretty fucked up too."

I heard Kevin and Veer's laughter come up the back stairs, and I sighed. It looked like the household was up and had probably heard the argument between Ashur and Tara.

"How do you do it? How do you pretend to be with one man when you're obviously in love with another?"

I glanced to the side and studied her. "We don't have a choice. There is too much at stake for all three of us."

"That's bullshit. We all have choices." Tara turned sad eyes on me. "We all make decisions, good or bad. I have to live with the ones I've made. You better get ready to live with yours."

"Don't you think I know this?" I heard the defensiveness in my tone as a lump formed in the pit of my stomach. My voice quivered as I asked, "Why can't I have him and my ambition?"

"Don't make the same mistake I did, Jacinta. I hurt

the only man I ever loved to protect my family and my future. I wish every day that I'd stood up to Minesh Kumar and told him to fuck himself. You're going to break Veer's heart. Once you take that path, you can't go back."

My own heart clenched. Tara was right. I wouldn't expect Veer to stay single once we separated. I shook my head, pushing the painful thoughts away.

"Jaci, I'm not trying to make it harder, but you have to know he will move on. He won't have a choice. Especially if Ashur breaks me down and gets what he wants me to..." She trailed off. "Never mind. It isn't my place to say this."

"Tara, what am I missing? What is Ashur asking you to do?"

"This is something I can't talk about. It is better that you find out from Veer or Ashur."

"Oh, believe me, I will." I frowned. Whatever this big secret was, I had a feeling it was going to be epic. Especially if Ashur went to all the trouble of crashing a party he wasn't invited to so he could meet with Tara.

"Would you be okay with me leaving?" Tara turned to me. "Ashur is part of your family, and I don't want to cause any more tension."

"You're part of the family too. If anyone is going to leave, it's Ashur. He showed up uninvited. Sisters before misters."

A slight grin touched Tara's lips. "Jacinta Camden, in all the years I've known you, you've never changed."

"Of course not. What would be the fun in that?" I

offered Tara my hand. "Come on. I know the perfect solution to stupid boy issues."

Tara lifted a brow. "And what's that?"

"Retail therapy. Let's grab Samina and leave the boys to do dumb boy stuff, like fishing. And if they're hungry, they can make their own breakfast. We can grab some brunch before we shop."

CHAPTER EIGHT

"I CAN'T BELIEVE you convinced Shawna to make you a custom dress," I said to Tara as we left Prima.

It was the design studio of Shawna Martinez. She had been my first ever client out of law school. A designer from a larger fashion house had stolen a collection when Shawna had applied for a job and shown her sketches for a new line of clothing. Shawna had sued for infringement of intellectual property and shed light on the practices of companies who poached on young designers. It had taken eighteen months of high media coverage and scrutiny, but in the end, we'd won her case with a hefty settlement.

Today she was one of the most sought-after designers who produced affordable, ready-to-wear clothing.

"I know—I can't believe it myself. I love Shawna's clothes, and it's almost impossible to get any pieces of her new collection," Tara said. "I'm so excited to have a closet full of her creations. Who knew she was such a fan of mine?"

My security guard, Oscar, opened the door to the limo for us, and we slid in.

"You seriously don't give yourself enough credit." Sam pulled out bottled waters, one for each of us. "You're a hero to so many people across the world. You're the badass who will look a human trafficker in the face without flinching."

"Well, the president made it seem as if I went behind his back and engaged in illegal negotiations."

"He's pissed that he looks like an ass for sitting back and letting you rescue seventy American teen girls from being sold as brides to men who wanted an easy way into the US."

There was a silent epidemic of poor immigrant families from the Middle East and Asia, where parents sold their daughters to wealthy men who were looking for a legal way into the United States. The girls had no choice in what happened to them, and if they refused, they were either thrown out of their homes or physically harmed. These parents viewed the dowry earned more than worth giving up a child to a man who could be three times their age.

It made my stomach turn to think of a thirteen-year-old girl having to marry a man in his fifties.

"I agree with Sam," I interjected. "You put a spotlight on something that was being ignored by the majority of the world. If I didn't have this senator gig, I would join you on your crusade."

Ever since what happened to me after Grey Decker Junior attacked me, I'd wanted to find a way to help those who were abused by the powerful. I'd thought running against these assholes was the way, but lately I was seeing the merits of using Tara's tactic of taking action and dealing with the consequences later. She had accomplished more in the past few years than I could have ever imagined.

"Jaci, the very man who ripped me a new one to the media is a member of your party. I never thought you'd go against the president." Tara furrowed her brow and gave me a look of disbelief.

"There are a lot of things I don't agree with him on." Among them the fact that he treated women as if their sole duty was to cater to men. "He may be the main party representative, but that doesn't mean he leads me around by the nose."

"Does he know this?" Sam asked while sipping her water. "He acts as if you're the daughter he's grooming to take his place."

"It's a game, Sam. You of all people should know how this works. Whatever I feel comes second to the end goal: me in the White House." I leaned back against the leather seat and kicked off my heels. "He, in all honesty, can't stand me. He's a childhood friend of Grey Decker and thinks I orchestrated the fall of both Decker Senior's and Junior's careers."

"Well, it takes one dipshit to defend another." Sam frowned. "To unseat men like them was the reason we went into politics, and now you're catering to one of them."

"That's not fair, and you know it. I don't have the freedom you do to oppose Edgar outright. My job is to play the chess game and let him think I'm a pawn. And then unseat him and let him realize I was the queen the whole time."

"Sorry, Jaci, but I'm not sure I can handle another four years of Edgar's shit."

I wanted to growl. If Edgar lost the election, then I'd have to go up against an incumbent when my time came, and that was always twice as hard to win, even more so if my challenger was a popular president.

"Don't scowl at me." Sam folded her arms across her chest. "I'm only stating what I feel. I don't have to be PC when it's just us."

Before I could respond, Tara spoke. "So, in other words, you and Edgar are using each other for political gain. He needs to improve his image with the nation and the more moderate Republicans after his antics this year, and having you as a member of his inner circle gives him an image of being more progressive. For you, it is all about getting him to position you as his successor since you need the support of the old-school party voters."

I sighed and set my water bottle in the holder. "Yep, that about sums it up."

"This is why I'd rather negotiate with terror groups. At least I know going in that they're the scum of the earth and I don't have to pretend to like them when we speak."

"Tara, some of the stuff you do scares the shit out of me." I studied the exhaustion still lingering on her face. "Please, for the sanity of everyone that loves you, no more secret meetings with known terrorists. Those men could have killed you. I'm afraid to ask what you did to get them to listen to a word you had to say."

"Things aren't cut and dry. Besides, I had help." Her eyes shifted to the window, and she stared out at the cars zooming past us. "I was never in the type of danger the president made it out to be. And I'd be damned if I was going to let another little girl marry some old man because of tradition."

"I'm sorry, Tara. I shouldn't have brought it up. I promised a relaxing weekend, and I'm failing miserably."

"It's okay." She turned back to me. "Today has been just what I needed."

Tara's phone chimed as did Sam's and mine.

"Okay, what's going on?" Sam pulled her mobile out of her purse.

I read through the messages my assistant Trisha was sending me and my heart sank, while a headache flared to life.

Images of Tara, Sam, and me were all over the Internet, and Decker had decided it was the perfect opportunity to hold a press conference discussing my questionable interaction with a liberal senator and an international activist with "possible" ties to terrorist organizations. He'd labeled me morally corrupt, and then there were posts about the president using his social media platform to support an investigation into our "secret" meeting. The fucking president was siding with Decker.

"Shit, fuck, shit." Sam ran a hand down her face. "Since when are lunch and shopping considered a secret meeting? I love you, Jaci, but this president has got to go."

"My sentiments exactly." Tara dropped her phone in her lap and pressed her fingers to her temples. "I'm so sorry I brought this on you."

"The hell you did. Tara, you may not believe it, but there are some of us who are loyal to you and will do what's necessary to make things right." I dialed Trisha's number. The second she answered, I said, "Call our contact with Mrs. Edgar. Tell her it's time to put the plan we discussed last week into action."

BY THE TIME WE REACHED HOME AN HOUR LATER, THE media surrounded the front gates of my estate, and my weekend respite from politics was shot, with no hope of recovery.

On the hour ride home, I'd filled Sam and Tara in on my idea to get the first lady on board as an advocate for Tara's cause. I told the girls Mrs. Edgar needed a project to show she was a separate person from her husband and his unpopularity, and by supporting the No Bride Initiative, she'd position herself as an advocate for women and Tara would no longer be labeled as someone who associated with terrorists but someone who fought against them.

I hadn't convinced either of them that my plan would work, but they'd agreed to let me work the angle.

"Oh God, they're everywhere," Tara exclaimed as we reached the entrance of my estate.

Media trucks and reporters lined the front gates, as did a crowd of people. Some with signs that said everything from "Tara the Hero" to "Camden associates with Terrorists."

My stomach hurt, knowing my parents would see all the coverage. At least I knew they'd support me without question.

I glanced at Tara. Her face was pale, and she looked as if she'd burst into tears.

Reaching over, I covered her hand with mine. "You did nothing wrong."

"I know, but I hate others using me for political gain."

"That's why we're going to fight this together." Sam laid her hand over ours. "This is how men like to play politics. Let's show them how women do it."

The glint in Sam's eyes told me she was on board with my plan. She knew as well as I did that the first couple couldn't stand each other and Mrs. Edgar was more than ready to stick it to her husband, even if she gave the public image of docile, subservient wife.

At that moment, the car paused in front of the house and Oscar opened our door. Five agitated men greeted us, scowls marring each of their faces as they stood on the front porch.

"Now if things weren't going to hell, I'd say that is

some delicious eye candy to come home to," Tara joked as she masked the pain that she'd been revealing only moments earlier.

"I'd say true, but I'm a married woman, and my eyes are only for the sexy federal judge glaring at me." Sam stepped out of the car and went toward Devin, who wrapped an arm around her.

Tara and I exited the limo after Sam.

To my surprise, Ashur came up to Tara and offered her a hand. "Let me help you, Tara."

She glanced at Veer, who inclined his head. After a few seconds, she nodded but didn't take the offered hand and walked past Ashur while saying, "Let's go inside, Ash. We have a lot to discuss. And I could use a stiff drink."

"Was I imagining that or was Mr. Moody being nice?" Kevin came up to me and draped an arm around my shoulder. "Well, nice for Ashur."

Veer remained on the porch with Tyler, glaring at us. I knew it was because of all the reporters with long-range camera lenses. However, I couldn't help but feel disappointed he hadn't come up to us.

"Don't frown. Remember the world is watching and you have to be happy to see me. Veer can cuddle you later."

"I don't think cuddling is on Veer's mind when he looks at my sister."

I heard the sound of a smack and glanced at the porch. Tyler rubbed the back of his head and scowled at Veer.

"What the fuck, man? Tell me you don't want to be the one standing next to her right now."

"Tyler, I'm going inside before I kill you in front of an audience." Veer turned and walked into the house.

"I swear he's been hanging out with our mom too much." Tyler continued to rub his scalp.

As Kevin and I climbed the stairs, Tyler's face grew serious. "I need you to do me a favor."

"That all depends on what you need me to do."

"Keep the military guys from orchestrating an attack on Decker while I make a few calls. I have a plan that will put that jackass Decker Senior in his place."

Kevin and I glanced at each other. Tyler was no longer the jokester. He'd put on his politician hat, which meant he was all business and ready to take action. I'd better rein him in before he got too far ahead of himself.

"Tyler, has Trisha sent you anything yet?"

"No, honestly I haven't paid attention. I'm more worried about helping you and the girls than talking to anyone outside of the estate." He clenched his jaw. "I am sick of that bastard fucking with my family."

"I think you need to breathe for a second. You're scaring me."

Tyler rarely, if ever, allowed his emotions to rule his actions, but when he got riled, he was hard to keep under control.

"You shouldn't be, but Grey Decker should be very scared." Tyler opened the door, letting Kevin and me enter the house.

I was positive that whatever Tyler was orchestrating would ruffle more than Decker's feathers. I'd better get the details before he implemented something that would cause me more pain than necessary.

I pulled both men to a stop, resulting in a frown from Tyler and a curious glance from Kevin.

"Kev, could you go and gather everyone in the library? I need to have a private word with my twin before I kill him."

"Glad it's you and not me." Kevin smirked and patted Tyler on the shoulder before he made a beeline down the hall.

After Kevin's footsteps quieted, I asked, "Ty, what are you planning? I think you should hold off for a second and let me fill you in on a few things."

He ignored me and tried to move around me, but I blocked his way. "I know you don't want anyone to know what happened to you, but other women are ready to come forward about Junior and his daddy. I think a few strategic leaks will shift the focus away from you, Sam, and Tara."

"No. Absolutely not!" I said, but Tyler ignored me, lifting me to the side and walking down the hall.

I stomped behind him, entering the library a few seconds after Tyler. "Dammit, will you listen for a damn minute? Tara, Sam, and I have it under control."

Sam sat on a nearby couch with her arms crossed and a pissed-off look on her face, Devin glared at Sam from his spot against the window, Veer fixed a drink at the bar in the back of the room, and Ashur and Tara were nowhere around.

"Have you heard the nonsense they've concocted?" I asked Sam.

"Oh, believe me. I have. These boys think we little women need them to rescue us. I think they forgot we could run circles around them when it comes to planning."

Devin clenched his jaw, stood, and moved to the bar cart where he poured himself a shot and drank it down. "I will do what is required to protect my wife and family."

"You will not leak anything," I said. "We did nothing wrong besides have lunch and shop. For your information, a plan is already in the works. I won't play this card unless it is undeniably necessary."

"It's necessary." Veer walked up, handing me a tumbler of scotch. "We've discussed it, and it is the best way to get the media sniffing in a different direction."

I cocked a hand on my hip and looked at Kevin, who stood just inside the doorway of the room. "Are you in on this too?"

"Yep." He gave me a determined stare. "The five of us had a long time to talk before your arrival. We agreed it's better to strike him where it hurts. This way he's too busy dealing with the fallout from his antics to worry about what you're up to."

A pulsing pain throbbed in my head, and my temper started to boil over. I loved these men, but hell would freeze over before I let them take over.

I growled at Kevin, "You're supposed to be on my side."

"I am, Jaci." He returned my scowl.

"I am only going to say this once. I love all of you for wanting to protect us, but a plan is already in the works, and you will not fuck it up. Do I make myself clear?"

Tara chose that particular moment to storm into the room, with Ashur steps behind her.

"Sam. If you want your brother alive, I suggest you keep him away from me. I don't give two shits if he is over a foot taller than me. I will kick him into the next century."

Sam shrugged. "Do what you have to. It may be better having one less stupid man in the room."

Ashur scowled at Sam. "Stay out of this, Samina."

"She's only stating the truth." Tara turned and poked a finger into Ashur's chest, which he grabbed. "Your method of help comes with too many strings, Ashur Kumar. The one time I needed you, you never came. The hell if I'll expect it now."

"You tell him, Tara. My brother is too big for his britches."

"Samina," Ashur warned, still holding Tara's hand, and then he said something in their family's native language of Gujarati that had Sam flipping him the bird and responding with a string of words I could only assume were insults.

"Do I want to know what she just called him?" Tyler looked at Veer.

"Nope," he responded with a smirk. "Sam, I know you didn't learn those words from your mom. You could put a sailor to shame."

Sam responded to Veer by switching languages to one I assumed was Tamil.

"Okay, okay. I'll leave you alone."

Veer's parents had immigrated to the US from South India before he was born and had taught their son their native language of Tamil. Then as he grew, they added English, Hindi, and Gujarati into the mix.

"I love that you guys are fluent in a million languages, but the non-Indian folk in the room can't understand you," I said, trying to break the tension.

Tara pulled her hand free of Ashur's hold. "She's only telling both of these overgrown apes that they are more than welcome to assist us, but if they even think to take over, then she is going to shove her foot so far up their asses that they won't be able to walk straight."

Tyler winced and then laughed as he saw the determined look on all of our faces. "Okay, Okay. I hear you."

"Ty, you may be the only one that does," I said, taking a seat between Sam and Tara.

"That's because I'm your twin. I know when you're going to kick my ass if I say anything else that you deem is stupid." He glanced at his phone, read the message, and then looked at me and lifted a brow.

He must have gotten the text I'd asked Trisha to forward to him, detailing the plan. Tyler had a handful of close friends who worked the White House and his connections would be the best bet to get the information we needed passed to Mrs. Edgar.

"Jaci." Tyler approached me and pulled me from my seat, hugging me tightly. "You're brilliant. Devious, but brilliant."

I relaxed into the comfort of his hold. "I am the genius in our family," I joked. "Will you help us and forgo the idiot plan you guys concocted?"

"I'll not only help you, but I'll play the middleman. I've just been asked to join the President's Council of Economic Advisers."

I kissed his cheek. "I can always count on you."

"Someone want to fill the rest of us in?" Devin asked. "I know you have that twin thing going, but the rest of us need complete sentences to understand each other."

I looked at Devin, then Ashur, and then Veer and Kevin. "My fabulous brother is going to help me put the president, and his cronies who've gone after Sam, Tara, and me in check."

CHAPTER NINE

I DANGLED my legs off the dock, kicking my feet back and forth and gazing at the river. The weather wasn't too hot or cold, and there was always a slight breeze coming off the water. God, I loved springtime in Austin.

I released a deep breath and sighed. My mind and body ached from the stress of the latter half of the day. It had taken a good two hours to get the rest of the guys to abandon their harebrained idea of outing the Deckers.

What they couldn't grasp was that the real enemy was the president. I was in a political chess game with him, and he thought he'd back me into a corner by supporting Decker's view on my outing with my friends. Eventually, everyone had agreed my plan had the most merit and would have the most impact. Thankfully, I'd gotten a discreet call from the first lady's assistant confirming a private meeting to bolster my stance.

What honestly sucked the most was filling Kevin in on

the real reason Decker and I hated each other. Reliving any telling of the incident hurt, but this time around, it wasn't as awful. I felt as if I'd worked through the demons and could view it more as a survivor than a victim. Maybe it was because I'd had years to work through the trauma, or maybe it was the fact that the closest people to me were in the room giving me strength.

Kevin's response had been similar to Veer's when he'd found out right before my election. He was ready to drive the four hours to Decker's estate and beat the living shit out of father and son. Once he calmed down, Kevin gave me his "we will talk later" look and shot back two fingers of cognac. I dreaded that conversation. It was another thing to add to my long list of keeping secrets from my unofficial/official boyfriend.

I shook my head. I had an incredible knack for hurting the two men who meant so much to me.

Sadness enveloped my heart. I'd leave for DC tomorrow, and things were unresolved between Veer and me. We'd barely had a moment alone since I'd arrived home and even then, it felt as if he was keeping his distance. Besides voicing his opinion here and there during our discussion of my plan, he'd said little to me. It was as if he was letting Kevin be the one who was supporting me.

Ashur was right about me having two men in love with me. But how could I explain that the love Kevin had for me was nothing like how it was with Veer without outing him?

Kevin came from a family and world where homosexuality wasn't accepted. His own mother would go into mini sermons condemning anyone who lived as an openly gay person. She'd tout the Bible and its teachings, constantly forgetting "to love your neighbor as you love yourself." I couldn't imagine how it must have felt growing up in a home where your parents believed sexual orientation was a choice.

A lump formed in my throat. Veer and I had to end. I made a promise to Kevin years before my relationship with Veer started. It was on this very dock that we'd set the arrangement that would benefit both of us. He would gain his inheritance and the family business, and I would have the husband and image needed to secure the nomination.

I knew deep down Kevin would never fault me for choosing Veer, but I refused to let the Deckers of the world win. Decker thought I was too weak to stand up to the pressures of politics. I couldn't believe the bastard had turned my outing with Samina and Tara as consorting with the liberal enemy. To top it off, the fucking jackass President Edgar hitting the social media circuit to voice his opinion.

This sucked.

I pinched the bridge of my nose. A migraine was flaring, and there was nothing I could do about it. Stress brought them on. My life was overflowing with it, and it wouldn't calm anytime soon.

Laughter sounded in the distance, and I knew the tension in the house had eased. Even Ashur and Tara had come to some truce. They weren't acknowledging each other or talking, but it was better than Tara threatening bodily harm.

A smile touched my lips, remembering how Tara had stormed into the room. When she said she'd knock Ashur on his ass, I had no doubt she could do it. Tara had secrets like the rest of us, but something about her said not to underestimate her abilities. If Ashur convinced Tara to do whatever it was he wanted her to do, Tara would make him regret ever asking her.

They still loved each other, even after over a decade since their breakup. However, the hurt caused by Ashur's father lingered like a chain anchoring them together.

I hoped one day they'd be able to handle encounters without pain lacing every interaction.

Would it be like that with Veer and me? Without a doubt, I knew no one would ever make me feel the way he did. He held my heart, and I held his. I only hoped we wouldn't move into anger. What I felt for Veer couldn't be defined—it was love, passion, and friendship all rolled together.

Footsteps echoed against the wooden planks of the pier, making me glance to my side. Veer walked up, wearing a pair of shorts and a loose linen shirt. His inky black hair was wet, fresh from a shower, and there was an intensity in the way he watched me as he came to stand behind me.

"Hi."

"Hi," I responded.

"Can I join you?"

We stared at each other for a moment before I nodded.

He sat down behind me with his legs draped along either side of mine. His body heat seeped into my back as he wrapped his arm around my waist and pulled me against him. For a split second, I wanted to shove him back and yell at him for ignoring me most of the evening, but another part of me understood why he had done it.

My lips trembled as my heart contracted in pain, knowing what was about to happen.

I released a deep breath and sank into his hold, trying to keep my emotions in check but failing miserably.

"It's time," he said in a gruff whisper filled with sadness.

"Please don't say it. I'm not ready."

"Why not? It doesn't change how things have to be. I heard what the first lady's assistant said to you. You have to announce your engagement soon to keep your plan in motion. I won't be the thing keeping you from your goal."

I turned, climbing onto his lap and straddling his firm thighs. I cupped his face and ran my thumb over his lips.

"Please."

Something flashed in his eyes, and then he closed them.

"Jaci."

I leaned my forehead against his. "Veer, just one more night."

He sighed and then nodded.

I slid my arms around his neck and leaned forward, sealing my lips against his. We kissed, trying to memorize every aspect of each other's mouths. Our tongues slid against each other's in a sensual dance, making my cleft dampen. He was an intoxicating blend of scotch and his own earthy flavor. I couldn't get enough of him.

A low moan escaped my lips as the familiar bulge of his cock pressed against my denim-covered crotch. I shifted my hips, trying to ease the arousal bubbling inside my core. One of his hands went to my hair, fisting it as he deepened our kiss, and the other went to my hip, grinding me harder along his erection.

"Veer," I murmured, not wanting to break the play of our mouths.

My nipples pebbled to stiff peaks against the lining of my bra, creating additional torture to the sensitive buds.

I shifted, rubbing my swollen pussy against his hard length, growing wetter and hotter. We were all but fucking each other, unable to stop the need consuming us. We were desperate, filled with hunger, passion, and love.

I wanted to memorize this night, to have it to remember that we were once more than the strangers we'd have to become, to remember what it was like to be deep-down, truly loved.

A tear slipped down my face, and Veer pulled back, breathing heavily.

"Baby, no. Think of nothing but now. There is no past or future, only the present."

At that moment a boat passed by, and hoots and laughter echoed from it, breaking the moment. I had no fear of being discovered since it was dark, but honestly, I didn't care. The love of my life was breaking up with me, and I only had this one night.

"Let's go inside. I don't want to share this with anyone," Veer said as he lifted me up. I adjusted my shirt and shorts, and Veer pulled out his tucked shirt to cover his erection.

We made our way back to the house, hand in hand, without saying a word. Our arousal hung heavily between us as we took the steps to my room.

Within seconds of my door closing, he had me pressed against it.

The need I felt for him was ten times more than anything I'd experienced before, and most of the time, I couldn't get enough of him.

I let out a small whimper as he cupped my breast, pinching the fabric-covered tip, and then bit my lower lip.

I pulled at the buttons of his shirt, struggling to get each one open so my fingers could stroke across his firm chest.

He stepped back, finishing the work I'd started, and then grabbed my tank, tearing it down the middle.

I gasped, and my heart skipped a beat seeing him stare at me with feral desire.

"Take it all off. If this is the last time I get you, I want nothing between us."

I swallowed, hating what awaited us come morning, and reached behind me to unlatch my bra. I pulled it free and dropped it to the ground. I pushed my shorts down my hips, taking my underwear with it.

I stood before him naked, desire flushing my skin.

"God, you're so beautiful. You take my breath away whether you're fully clothed or without a stitch on."

"You aren't bad yourself. Planning on joining me?"

"Oh, I plan to, but it can wait. I want to hear my name on your lips at least three times before I bury myself inside you."

"Feeling confident, aren't you?"

A slight grin touched his face. "I've never heard you complain that I haven't followed through on my promises."

If there was one thing Veer was known for, it was his commitment to his promises.

"Give me all you've got."

"Oh, I plan to." He came toward me with a wicked grin, but then picked me up and laid me carefully on the bed as if I were so precious he was worried I'd break.

I ran my thumb across his bottom lip. He lowered his head, kissing my neck, and he tongued down my throat and between my breasts before he moved to a taut, swollen nipple. He teased and tormented, drawing circles round and round. My body shuddered, and my breath quickened.

"Oh God," I gasped and clenched Veer's thick hair with my fingers.

He growled in response and then moved to my other aching bud, engulfing it in his mouth and nipping the tip with his teeth.

My core quickened, and my entire body tightened.

His hand rubbed up and down my side, sending

goosebumps all over my body. "Can you come for me like this, baby?"

"I..." was as far as the words got as he pulled on my nipple with deep, hard sucks, sending me over.

I called out his name, thrashing my head back and forth while gripping tighter on Veer's inky strands.

"That's it, love. Now let me hear you again."

He slid lower, rubbing his beard down my abdomen until he reached my still-pulsing pussy. He blew against my soaked cleft and then took a long, deep swipe with his tongue.

"You taste delicious." He licked again. "I'll never get enough of you."

"More." I lifted my hips toward his mouth.

"Patience." He shifted my legs to around his shoulders. "The best things come to those who wait."

"I hate waiting," I complained.

"Believe me." He spread my cleft, exposing my swollen clitoris and then circling it with his tongue. "I know this."

"Vveeer..." I shuddered as each stroke sent me closer and closer to another orgasm. My hold tightened on Veer's scalp.

He pushed a finger into my pussy and rubbed against the sensitive spot deep in my core. My toes curled, and my body squirmed with each thrust of his delicious tongue.

"Come for me, baby," he said, increasing his rhythm.

On command, every muscle in my body seized to an almost painful pleasure and my back bowed.

I cried out, tumbling into a freefall of exquisite

sensation. My pussy spasmed and clenched around his thrusting digit and tongue.

As my body slowly came down from its release, he began the climb again, using his mouth to fuck my core, mimicking the deep thrusts of his fingers. I came almost immediately, screaming my pleasure.

"That's three, love."

"Yes, it is." I half gasped, half laughed. "You always keep your promises, Governor George."

His head rose, locking his gaze with mine. He took one last taste of my clit and crawled over me, hovering with his arms on either side of my head. His hard cock dripped his arousal along my slick cleft. I squirmed, lifting my spread thighs.

"How bad do you want me?" he asked as he stared at me. His eyes filled with love and a touch of sadness.

I cupped his cheek. "More than you could ever know."

He lowered his head, sealing his mouth across mine, sliding his tongue past my lips. I moaned, tasting my own essence. My nipples tightened further as they rubbed against the light dusting of hair on his chest.

He took hold of one of my hands, pinning it above my head, and then repeated the action with the other. We continued to kiss and savor each other's mouths.

All of a sudden, I felt the familiar press of Veer's cock push past my cleft and slide deep into my pussy.

I broke our kiss and cried out, "Veer."

He pulled out to the tip of his bulbous head and

slammed back in, hoisting my body upward onto the bed. He rolled his hips and held himself deep.

My arousal flooded around him, and my desire became almost too painful to handle.

"I need..."

He rubbed his pelvis against my clit. "I know what you need. I've always known what you needed."

He touched his forehead to mine. I tugged my hands free of his grip and wrapped them around his neck.

His cock pulsed against the swollen walls of my core, prompting me to say, "I need you to fuck me."

The sadness vanished from his eyes and was quickly replaced by amusement.

"You're in no position to make demands." He pulled out and then pressed back in. "Want it slow or fast, Jaci?"

A quiver shot through me, making me gasp. "Whatever you want as long as you make me come."

"That's the plan. How about three more?"

I knew better than to question his ability and said, "Go for it."

A big smile appeared on his face. "I love you, Jacinta Camden."

"I love you, Veer George. Now fuck me." I dug my fingers into his shoulders.

He growled and set a pace that had me building instantly, pussy quivering and body contracting. He rode me hard, bringing me from one orgasm to another and another. He held nothing back, telling me without words how much he wanted and needed me.

When I couldn't take another release, he came, in a deep, powerful shudder, saying, "You will forever be mine."

After a few minutes, Veer turned us so I was draped across him but kept his cock pulsing inside me.

I watched the fall and rise of his chest and felt an ache inside mine. I didn't want us to end. If only there were other options that would allow us to have what we both wanted. I held in the tears that burned the back of my eyes and released a breath, lifting my head to look at him.

He cupped my face and opened his mouth to speak, but I covered it.

"Tonight, there is nothing but us. No politics, no careers, no plans for the future."

The clench of his jaw said he wanted to argue, but then he conceded, nodding and then rolling me onto my back and thrusting deep once again.

CHAPTER TEN

Around seven in the morning, I leaned against my kitchen island, sipping a cup of robust coffee. My heart felt ripped to shreds.

After making love to me one last time, Veer had slipped from the bed, kissed my forehead, and whispered, "I'll love you until the day I die. Be happy, Jaci. I'll always be out there cheering for you."

I wanted to grab him and pull him back. To tell him I didn't want us to end. To tell him I didn't want to live a life without him. But I hadn't. I'd let silent tears fall as he dressed and walked out of my life.

I knew I'd see him at political events or family gatherings with Sam, but it would never be the same. I wouldn't have the right to ever touch him or kiss him the way I wanted to.

What was going to kill me was the day I'd meet the

woman who could give him everything he'd wanted from me: a wife, children, and family.

My throat burned with tears, and I inhaled deep to hold them back.

"Where's Veer?"

I turned to look at Samina as she sleepily walked into the kitchen and headed for the French press.

"Why would I know?"

She gave me an annoyed glare and poured herself a large mug of the piping-hot brew.

"You two were going at it all night. I assumed you would know where the man who screwed your brains out was."

My cheeks heated.

"I guess we were pretty loud?"

"It wasn't that bad. Nothing more than what you heard when Devin would come to visit us when we were in school."

"Oh God." I ran my hand down my face. "That means half the house heard us. Why do you think I conveniently found a way to make a trip home whenever Big Brother planned to come into town?"

"Whatever. We weren't that bad. Besides, I can say without a doubt, the governor of Texas has more stamina than Dev. And I didn't think anyone could outdo him."

I bit my lip, trying to hide my embarrassment. "You won't have to worry about noises from my room anymore. Those days are over."

I set my cup on the counter and stared out the window.

"You broke up with him?" Sam came to stand next to me.

I shook my head. "It was the other way around."

"Oh Jaci." Sam rested her head against the side of my shoulder. "He loves you. It's written all over his face every time he glances your way."

"He wanted marriage and babies. I wanted it too, but it would have cost me everything."

"Like I said the other day, I'm not judging you. I know better than most that politics is twice as brutal when it comes to women."

"Sometimes I wish we would have broken up years ago. Then it wouldn't hurt as much."

"It would have hurt regardless of when it happened. For the record, if you'd told me about the two of you from the beginning, I would have advised you on all the issues of falling in love with a liberal-leaning, dominant technology billionaire turned real-estate tycoon. After all, he is my adopted brother."

"Why can't a woman have her ambition *and* the man?"

"She can, but not without compromises."

I glanced at Sam. She had a hand on the delicate swell of her belly. She and Devin had gotten their second chance because they had met in the middle. Never would I have ever thought my ultra-driven brother, who'd gained a position as a federal judge by the time he was thirty, would step down from the judicial bench to let Samina pursue her political career.

"Maybe one day you'll find your way back to each other," Sam added.

I shook my head. I couldn't pretend. "No, we won't. He wants the family he's always dreamed of having. He's a marry-once-and-forever kind of guy." I turned toward Sam. "Do me a favor."

She looked up at me. "What?"

"Don't set him up with anyone I know. He'll come to you to help him find the right girl."

With Veer's looks and money, he could find the wrong girl all day and night.

"You're the right girl. Anyone else is just a consolation." Sam wrapped her arms around me. "I promise. Why don't you go sit outside while I make some tea and then I'll join you?"

With a nod, I grabbed my cup from the counter and headed out the door leading to the patio.

As I made my way down the wraparound deck of the house, I came to a halt. Ashur paced back and forth as he dialed someone on the phone. His face was in a hard scowl.

It was too early for Tara to have done something to piss him off, and as far as I knew, she wasn't awake yet. She'd told me she wanted one more day of sleeping in before she had to return to Seattle and take on her new caseload.

"Where the fuck are you? We were supposed to talk

this morning." Ashur cupped the back of his neck. "I don't care if it is the crack of dawn. We have shit to discuss."

It was probably business. It took a force of nature to get him to step away from his many business endeavors. Ashur had a head for finance and technology that had allowed him to create one of the top private equity firms in the country.

A little less than ten years ago, he, Kevin, Veer, and Devin had started mining bitcoins. In the beginning, it was all for fun to see if the tech skills each of them had could get them some pocket change but quickly it had turned into more, netting them hundreds of thousands of dollars. Once huge bitcoin farms became commonplace, the market became too volatile. So the group decided to sell the cryptocurrency for stocks and real estate. This led all of them to become independently wealthy. Ashur had used his funds to help technology startups as an angel investor, leading him to earn a return ten times his initial contribution.

Ashur set the phone on the railing and hit the speaker button. I was about to let him know I was there, when he said, "Veer, I'm in. No more exploring. Now you need to do your part."

This was about the big secret Veer and Tara had been keeping. No one would tell me what it was when I'd asked, so I guessed snooping was the next best option, and I had no guilt whatsoever.

"Ash, you need to calm the fuck down unless you want

to make an official declaration. Someone is bound to hear you."

Declaration? What were they planning?

"No one's up, so stop your worrying." He glanced at his watch. "Fuck. It's seven. I thought it was earlier. Samina will be up, and if she learns our plan before I talk to her, she's going to castrate me, and whether or not Tara agrees won't matter."

Then Ashur picked up his phone and began to scroll through some pictures. Over his shoulder, I could see that he'd stopped at one of Tara. She was lounging by the pool with shades covering her eyes. It was from two nights ago. He traced her face with his finger.

I shook my head. He had been such an ass to her and now he was longing for her.

"Why did you convince me to come down? We haven't settled anything, and Tara can barely stand to be in the same room with me, much less want to be the mother of my children."

Veer laughed over the line. "So, no thawing the glacier of ice between you two?"

He set the phone back on the railing and gripped it. "That would be an understatement. I've avoided Tara for over a decade, pushing down the hurt, and now a few days in her presence and my mind is all jacked up, and all I can think about is everything that kept us apart for a decade. I wish one of us had stayed away."

"In her defense, Tara had no idea you were coming. She is Samina and Jacinta's friend. She planned the trip months ago. Besides, she needed a break from all the media attention she's gotten recently because of the misogynist in the Oval Office."

I internally shook my head. Veer always had a knack for throwing in a jab at the president.

"Who told her to get involved with that organization? She shouldn't have put herself in such a dangerous position." A small tic pulsed on the side of Ashur's face. "They could have killed her."

"She started the organization, idiot. Of course, she's going to be involved. You can't change who she is. Her life means nothing if she doesn't try to save the innocent. That's the reason you need her to accomplish your plan."

Ashur's hold on the railing tightened. "I don't need her. She'll become a liability if she keeps pursuing her agenda. I can do it without her."

"The hell you can. She is your ace in the hole. Without her, no one from the left will take you seriously. She's an international phenomenon."

After a long pause while Ashur stared at Tara's picture, he said, "Fine. Make it happen."

"And how do you suppose I do this? If you recall, she told you to go fuck yourself."

"Those weren't the words she used."

"It was close enough."

"Whatever. You going to help me or not?"

"I'll give it a shot, but remember you don't have much to bargain with. You need her more than she needs you."

Ashur released a frustrated breath. "Use my money.

She needs funding for her projects. I don't care if you promise her half my net worth. It's not as if I'll spend it in this lifetime or the next."

"So in other words, you're going to buy her?"

"It's a mutually beneficial business decision. She gets unending funding to save the world and I get a wife who will endear herself to the masses. Just make sure you don't forget to detail expectations on both our parts in a thorough contract. I don't want any misunderstandings."

"You're the only man who could make marriage to the only woman he's ever loved into a business decision."

"That's all it is. The past is the past. Tara made a choice when she left."

"That's bullshit, and you know it. After everything that happened this weekend, I can't believe you'd hold on to old mistakes and hurts. You know the truth, and you're still hiding your head in the sand from it. She was innocent. You want a villain, then look at your father. He's the bad guy in this, not Tara."

"Stay out of it, Veer. Why don't you figure out how to handle your conservative princess and how she's going to react instead of giving me unsolicited advice?"

Unfazed by Ashur's jab, Veer responded, "It's not unsolicited if I'm doing your work for you. Your ass should be the one proposing to Tara. If we win, I can almost see how it will look when the first lady tells the world the vice president was the one who proposed to her instead of her husband."

"Funny, asshole. At least Tara likes you and will

consider anything you offer her. If I went to her she'd slam the door in my face before I got one word out." Ashur sighed. "This isn't how I thought I'd marry her, but at least I'll have her."

My stomach burned as I realized exactly what Veer and Ashur were orchestrating. Tears filled my eyes. I couldn't believe this was their secret. Why hadn't I figured it out? The clues were everywhere.

"Well, as you said, you'll still have her."

Ashur checked his watch again. "V, make it happen. I have to go talk to Sam and fill her in."

"Good luck."

"I'm not the one that will need the luck. We're about to take the wind from Jacinta's sails."

"She'll understand." Veer paused. "At least, I hope she will when she hears about it."

"You aren't going to tell her?"

"We broke up."

"What? You love her. Why the fuck would you do that? I thought I was the moron out of the two of us."

"It's better to cut it off completely." Veer's voice was gruff as he responded. "The longer I waited, the harder it was."

He was hurting as much as I was.

"Shit. I'm sorry, man."

"As I said, it's for the best."

"I guess. I'll talk to you on my drive back to Houston. Time to go face the Samina tiger and hope she doesn't eat me for breakfast." Ashur pressed the off button on the phone and then gazed out to the water.

After a few moments, he turned and walked inside the house. I quickly pressed myself against the wall and stayed out of sight.

My mind reeled. What was I going to do?

With Tara, there was no way Ashur wouldn't win. He was too conservative for a so-called Independent, even with Veer's liberal-leaning tendencies on his ticket. It was Tara who would show he was more than a politician.

Tara had endeared herself to the younger demographic of the nation. Because of her, there had been an influx of people joining humanitarian efforts, not only in the US but all over the world. Her international popularity would open doors our current president had shut because of his antics.

My hands shook as a sense of betrayal settled on my shoulders. Ashur and Veer were positioning themselves for a ruthless fight for the presidency. They were checking all the boxes to win.

Veer had held this secret close to his chest for months. There was no way a decision like this was spur of the moment. We were lovers, friends, and I thought so much more.

If he and Ashur won, I'd go up against them in four years.

I pressed my palms to my eyes, letting my tears drip down my cheeks. Ashur was taking my dream and making it his. And on top of that, Veer was helping him do it.

How could they do this to me?

How could the man I loved position himself between me and the one thing I'd spent my life working toward?

Accepting Ashur's proposal was the reason Veer had made the final decision to end us. He was on a timeline. It was either I gave up my ambition for him, or we broke up.

No, that wasn't fair. Veer had wanted me to marry him a year into our relationship, and he'd never once told me I had to give up the future I'd planned.

Oh God, why hadn't I said yes? Then we wouldn't be in this situation.

Inhaling deep, I reined in my emotions and thought of a game plan. First, I was going to have my tea with Sam and enjoy her company for the short time we had left together. Then, I was going to tend to my guests before we said our goodbyes. Finally, when it was just Kevin and me left, we were going to re-strategize our game plan for the next few months. This news would affect him as well. And if there was one thing we were good at, it was adjusting our plans for the future.

CHAPTER ELEVEN

Two weeks after leaving Austin, I exited my car at the basement entrance of the Rosewood Washington Hotel in the heart of Washington DC. Ashur had yet to make his big announcement, something I knew would occur any day.

I'd spoken with Samina in great detail about what was going to happen, and I'd resolved myself to the fact that more than likely I'd go up against Ashur in four years. It hurt deep inside to know people who I considered family would become my enemies. No matter how we felt behind closed doors, in public, we'd have to stay strictly along party lines. The worst part was my best friend would side with her brother and I couldn't expect anything else of her.

Then there was Veer. I hadn't heard from or spoken to him since he left my house that weekend. The only news I'd heard about him was when Veer had ruffled a few feathers in Texas by repeatedly voicing his opposition to the president's spending bill, especially his handling of education funding for states falling behind the national average. Veer and I had conflicting views when it came to government spending, but education was an issue we agreed on. Texas was almost at the bottom of the list on education, and our state needed to increase funding for public schools.

A few of my colleagues had given me the side eye when I informed them I wouldn't be voting in support of the president's spending bill. I may have been his public protégé but I wasn't his puppet, and people were going to know it.

Releasing a sigh, I focused on the guards approaching me. There was no point in wallowing in a situation that I had no control over. At this moment, I had more important things to handle.

Spreading my hands out, I waited for security to frisk me and then take me inside.

"Senator Camden, Mrs. Edgar is waiting for you. As you were informed earlier, no one is to know this meeting occurred," the first lady's secretary, Mary Davis, said the moment I passed through the doors.

"This shouldn't be a problem since any news of this would be detrimental to both of us."

She was protective of her boss, something I could respect. Mrs. Amanda Edgar had endured humiliation and criticism that would have destroyed a weaker woman. She'd experienced the plight of many women who thought they had a loving and committed marriage only to learn it was all one-sided. Except, the first lady's was through a public discovery.

The news of the affair broke during a family vacation the president and the first lady had taken with their adult children. A national newspaper reported the president had had a five-year affair with his assistant and had only ended it weeks before taking office. Mrs. Edgar was further embarrassed to learn everyone around her had covered it up.

She'd held her head high, knowing that divorce wasn't an option until the president left office without causing more scandal. Instead, she threw herself into projects that meant something to her, everything from childhood literacy to women's health. Her work was the only saving grace for the current administration.

"This way. We have a long walk, but it is necessary."

I nodded again and followed Mary through a back hallway in the basement of the hotel. After clearing two more hallways and climbing three sets of stairs, we reached a room guarded by six Secret Service agents. One of them nodded to Mary and then opened the door.

I followed Mary inside to find more agents in the corners of the classical French-designed room and the striking first lady sitting by the fireplace while sipping a cup of tea. Her long blond hair was tucked into a loose but stylish bun and her baby-blue day suit accentuated her fit form. She was anything but an aging woman in her early sixties. She had the appearance and physique of a woman twenty years younger. The only things that showed her years were her green eyes. They were filled with knowledge and sadness.

"Mrs. Edgar, thank you for meeting with me." I offered her my hand, and she stood, taking it.

"Jacinta, it is so good to see you." She kissed my cheeks, released my hand, and gestured to a seat next to her. "Come sit. We have a lot to go through in a short amount of time."

I took my place in the antique armchair and pulled out two folders, handing one to the first lady and placing the other one on my lap. "These are the logistics we discussed in detail. It has the timeline of negotiations Ms. Zain was involved in, as well as everyone she encountered. We've put in a date that we suggest you say was when you became involved in the No Bride project."

"Since Mary was part of the planning, I'm sure it is exactly what I requested. It's a shame Ms. Zain isn't here— I would have loved to meet the legend in person. However, I completely understand her wanting to keep the spotlight away from us."

"Once you make the announcement that No Bride will become your project, it will take the president's focus off her and end the push for a probe into her actions."

A frown touched her face. "Henry has a way of turning the scrutiny away from his actions and toward those of others. I should know—he threw me to the media and had them question why I accepted his infidelity, instead of admitting he was wrong." There was a bitterness laced with sadness in her tone that made me want to hug her.

I remembered a recent conservative news broadcaster who said the first lady was a terrible role model to young women for putting up with the president's affair. I couldn't believe the reporter's words. He completely ignored the fact she was a victim of the situation and tried to make her a villain.

"It is easy to criticize when they aren't in your shoes. We live in a world of double standards."

"Thank you for that." She patted my hand. "Now let's get to the nitty gritty and finalize how we're going to stick it to my husband and come out smelling like roses."

I laughed and started detailing every step of the next few weeks.

A FEW DAYS AFTER MY MEETING WITH THE FIRST LADY, Trisha walked into the living room of my DC townhouse with a large bouquet of roses and a gift box.

"Senator, these arrived for you."

"Who are they from?" I asked, but I knew who sent them. If there was one thing Kevin was good at, it was remembering special days. Plus, he was due any minute to take me out to dinner.

"It says a secret admirer." She smiled.

I frowned. Kevin never addressed himself like that. If he were going to write anything, it would be something with a bit of humor, like, "From your sexy frog turned prince."

I stood up from my couch, placing my book on the side table, and moved toward Trisha. "Set them on the coffee table."

"I have to say you are one lucky lady with Kevin Stanton. He's gorgeous, successful, and adores you. He's going to make this birthday special."

I nodded and picked up the card, seeing it was the exact message Trisha had said. Then I opened the gift. As the paper came loose, my heart began to pound into my ears.

Oh God, he wouldn't. I reached in and pulled out a ruby-and-diamond-encrusted key. Tears filled my eyes as the memory of something Veer had said to me years ago when we were friends and nothing more surfaced.

The one I fall in love with will hold the key to my heart until the day I die. Even if we go our separate ways, she will be the only one for me.

My fingers shook around the pendant. Veer had known I'd remember. I remembered everything.

Oh, Veer.

"Wow. That's the Tiffany Keys Round Star pendant. It's like fifteen thousand dollars."

I remained quiet, staring at the gems twinkling against the light.

Trisha must have picked up on my melancholy because she set her hand over mine. "I'm sorry. I shouldn't have assumed it was from Mr. Stanton."

"It's okay."

"If it makes you feel better, Governor George isn't doing much better without you."

My gaze shifted to Trisha's. She'd known about Veer and me from the time our affair started. Even if I'd thought to keep it from her, there was no hiding what I was doing. Trisha knew the ins and outs of my life better than I did.

"How would you know?"

"We assistants talk, and Abigail, Governor George's, said he spends most of his free time holed up with Mr. Kumar or brooding while staring at a picture of you he keeps hidden in his office."

I swallowed the lump in my throat.

"Would you mind giving me a few minutes alone? I need to get myself together." As she turned toward the door, I added, "Also, will you tell Bridget to get the guest room ready? Mom and Dad will be staying with me for a few weeks until the end of renovations on their townhouse."

Trisha nodded and left, closing the door behind her.

I picked up my phone from the side table and dialed Veer's number.

"Senator Camden," he said in his deep, raspy timber. "What can I do for you?"

"Vee...Governor George." My voice cracked. "How are you?"

"Busy. Was there a reason you called?" he asked coolly.

"I wanted to say thank you for my gift."

"You're welcome. Happy birthday, Senator Camden."

What was with the Senator Camden references? Even if we weren't together, I'd thought we'd be friendly if not friends.

"Why are you being so formal?"

"Because it's the way it has to be. Ashur filed today. You and I are no longer on the same side."

His words were like a slap to my face. My body shook as I sat down on the sofa.

"Then why did you send me something that would rip me apart?"

"It wasn't meant to be…"

I cut him off. "You knew I would remember. Damn you." Tears streamed down my face. "I'd rather you not contact me at all."

"Fuck. Jaci. Please don't hang up," I heard, just as I pushed the end button.

Dropping my phone on the couch, I folded my legs under me and sobbed, still clutching the key held tight in my palm.

This separation hurt more than I'd ever thought possible. I missed Veer so much. Why had I called him?

For the past weeks, I'd kept my mind off Veer by throwing myself into work and the plan with the first lady. It was only when I was alone or when I found something he'd left behind in a random spot, like his cufflinks in the townhouse, that the sadness would come back full force. Now I was left with collecting everything and putting it away so I wouldn't have to see it again.

"Baby girl, what's wrong?"

Stiffening, I glanced at my father, who stood in the doorway of the living room. He held a tuxedo jacket over one arm, and his tie was unknotted and lying on his shoulder. The worried expression on his face made me want to crawl onto his lap as I'd done when I was a little girl for comfort. Dad was a hardnosed politician, but with me, he was always my daddy, who would jump at the chance to slay my dragons.

I gave him a tight smile and then gazed down at the diamond pendant.

He came to sit next to me on the sofa. He took my hand in his and then the key from my palm. He turned it over and saw the inscription I'd missed earlier.

My heart forever.

Fresh tears surfaced, making me wipe at my cheeks.

"Jacinta, if you ever want to win the election in four years, if you ever want to have any hope of becoming president, you can't go back with him."

My gaze shifted from the pendant to Dad's knowing eyes.

"Don't look at me that way. I've known you've been together for years. I have no idea what broke you up, but it's for the best. I'm not blind. That man loves you, and for some reason, he gave you up. Think of it as a blessing."

"I wish I could," was all I said.

"Kevin is the right choice for you. I know you care for each other and that he's very protective of you. Maybe, given some time, you'll grow to love him. Having him by your side will give you a solid foundation, and in four years, you'll be a shoo-in for the party's nomination."

"Dad, I don't think I'll ever get over Veer." I rested my head on his shoulder as his arm came around me, pulling me to his side. "And I know I'll end up hurting Kevin in the long run. He deserves better than me, but he is willing to ride this crazy train to the White House."

"Does Kevin know about you and Veer?"

I nodded. "Yes."

"And he's okay with it?" The disbelief was obvious in his voice. My dad was an alpha male who'd never stand for his woman seeing anyone else.

"We don't have a traditional relationship. It is more a friendship."

Dad shook his head. "I will never understand this. That boy is a great young man. It makes no sense why he'd let you have a full-blown affair with another man."

"Umm." I had no idea what to say. This conversation had just turned awkward, and I cringed. At least it kept me from falling apart all over my daddy.

"Does Kevin have someone?"

"Yes."

"Then why are you a couple? This type of relationship makes no sense. Jacinta Ellen Camden, we raised you to follow your dreams, not settle."

"I have no choice. To achieve the dream I had since I was little, I had to settle in my personal life."

"So, it's all about politics?"

"No." I shifted on my seat. "There are reasons why

135

Kevin and I are together that have nothing to do with my ambition."

He paused, his lips thinning for a second, and then he said, "Whatever it is, don't let anyone think you're anything less than a genuine couple. Edgar will use anything to discredit you. Right now, if he said anything against you, it would backfire. People think politics is about fighting the opposing party—but no, it's about fighting your own."

"The act is something Kevin and I have mastered. I'm sure it will continue into our marriage." My stomach hurt just thinking about that. Kevin and I deserved to be with the ones we loved.

"I don't like this. I'd rather you be single than in a marriage of convenience where the two of you have affairs on each other. I want you to have what Devin has with Samina and what I have with your mother."

"I want that too." I sighed. "But it's just not in the cards for me. At least I'm going to spend my days with someone I respect and is my friend."

We sat in silence for a few minutes, then Dad turned to me. "Jaci, you were always so determined, so special. I'm worried you are going to lose a piece of yourself trying to get the presidency."

"I have lost a piece of myself." I took the key from Dad's hand and traced the inscription with my thumb. "Now it's time to focus on the end goal. Things are about to happen that will pit those inside the White House against each other. I'll need your support, connections, and guidance to navigate it."

He kissed the top of my head. "Does it have to do with Tara Zain and your secret meeting with the first lady?"

I gave him the side eye. "Tyler told you. He's my twin, and he can't keep a secret worth anything."

"No, it was Samina. She wanted me ready to back you when Edgar publicly turned on you."

"She's definitely a Camden, sticking her nose into everything."

"That's why we love her. She'll fight for those she loves, even if they are on different party lines. Now, why don't you fill me in on the details so that I can rally some support without the doofus finding out."

I laughed and shook my head, feeling some of my sadness wane. "It's not nice to call names. Isn't he your friend?"

"Like they say. Keep your friends close, but your enemies closer."

CHAPTER TWELVE

"HEY, beautiful. Ready to party it up?" Kevin said as he entered my townhouse three weeks after my birthday. "We've got two nights of back-to-back events."

He was dressed to the nines tonight in a custom-made black-and-gray shawl-lapel tuxedo and his white-blond hair was in a slightly messy style, giving him a rakish appearance. He carried a big box wrapped in light-pink paper with a giant fuchsia bow on top.

I folded my arms across my chest and glared at him. "You stood me up for my birthday."

"Sorry, I had no choice. I was in the middle of negotiations. Let me say for the record, I'd rather have spent my time with you than on a flight to West Africa."

"Promise to make it up to me this weekend, and I'll forgive you." I smiled.

Following tonight's gala, Kevin and I planned to drive to NYC. We had to attend a giant bipartisan charity fundraiser and thought to make it into a fun trip instead of all business. I hated all the back-to-back events, but it couldn't be helped. This was a national election year, and every Tom, Dick, or Harry with political ties wanted to throw a gala. And it would look very bad for the party if the "Republican Darling," as the media had dubbed me, didn't attend the bigger ones.

Plus, a trip to the Big Apple with Kevin would give us the perfect opportunity to create a fairy-tale proposal. Especially since the media was expecting an engagement announcement any day.

"Will telling you that you look stunning tonight start the process?"

I glanced down at my Elie Saab black-and-gold high-slit gown.

"It's a start."

"I think this will get me back in your good graces sooner rather than later."

He handed me the box, and I couldn't help but squeal a little. Kevin had gift-giving down to a science, and I knew whatever was inside would be amazing.

"Damn, this is heavy." I set my clutch and the box on the sideboard and began tearing at the pink paper.

When I opened the lid, tears burned my eyes. "Oh my God, you didn't." I carefully pulled out a Chihuly one-of-a-kind blown-glass sculpture. Blue, red, and gold shot out from the center, like fire trying to reach outward, and at the bottom it said, "Jacinta, never stop aiming for the sky."

A hiccup escaped my lips. I had fallen in love with

Chihuly's unique style of artwork years ago on a trip I'd taken with friends to St. Thomas. The hotel we stayed at had ceilings made with Chihuly's glass masterpieces. I always said I'd have one of his creations in my house, and now I would.

"How did you get him to do this? I thought he rarely did commissions nowadays?"

Kevin approached me, taking the piece from my hands and walking to my office, where he placed it on the large window table next to my favorite reading chair.

"You know these things I am involved in called resorts? Well, my hotel group commissioned Chihuly to design the ceiling of the casinos in two of our new properties."

I wrapped my arms around him, hugging him tight. "You're the best."

He held my waist and squeezed. "Back at you."

He pulled from me and offered me his arm. "Ready to enjoy an evening with the Washington elite?"

"Not really." I slipped my hand through his. "I hate galas. If you've been to one, you've been to all. I'd rather sit on the back porch and stare at the stars."

"How about this? We'll mingle for a few hours, make up some excuse to escape the festivities, and then spend the evening here relaxing. This way we can get in a few hours' sleep, hit the road before dawn, and make it to New York just in time for all the shops and attractions to open up."

His idea had merit. "What excuse will we give?"

"Let's leave it open so everyone can jump to conclusions."

"I think that's the perfect plan. Time to go, Mr. Stanton."

"After you, Senator."

———

WE ARRIVED AT THE NATIONAL BUILDING MUSEUM for the Charityworks Dream Ball a little before seven. Cars lined the driveway, and we had to pass through at least three security checkpoints.

A tinge of anxiety fluttered in my stomach. This would be the first time I'd see Veer since Ashur had made his announcement three weeks ago. The media had taken to Ashur like moths to flames, including many straight Republican voters. Ashur leaned conservative enough to appeal to them, and his military record made the president look like a draft dodger. Then when he introduced Tara as his fiancée, the younger voting demographic jumped to support Ashur's ticket.

I still couldn't believe Veer had convinced Tara to marry Ashur. He must have offered literally half of Ashur's wealth, which I knew was in the billions and would fund Tara's efforts for the rest of her life. What I worried about was the emotional turmoil both Ashur and Tara would take on to keep their marriage a business deal, when both of them were still in love with each other.

Now with Tara by Ashur's side, all he had to do was

declare his running mate, but everyone knew it would be Veer.

Kevin and I approached the attendant who gave us entrance into the building.

"I'm setting my timer." Kevin lifted his wrist and turned something on his platinum Patek Phillipe watch. "In three hours exactly, we'll make our escape. Ready?"

"I was born ready."

"Believe me, I know this, Senator Camden."

We followed a long hallway that led to a large space converted into a ballroom. The second we entered, an awareness rippled down my spine, and my heart skipped a beat.

I turned and saw Veer standing with a group of congressmen and women. They were in a deep discussion, but I was positive he was completely in tune with my presence. It was always like this whenever we were in the same room.

"Are you okay?" Kevin set his hand on my back and glanced in the same direction I was looking. "You knew he'd be here."

"I know. It's just hard not to feel like a rejected, lovesick puppy."

He squeezed my waist. "You and me both. At least we have each other."

"True." I smiled at a group of people who walked by us. "I don't see Ashur and Tara."

Tara and I hadn't spoken about the new phase of her

relationship with Ashur. The only thing she'd told me was that there were reasons why she agreed to marry Ashur that made it worth it in the long run. When I'd questioned her about their sex life, she'd laughed and said there wasn't one. They were embarking on a political marriage and nothing more.

I hoped she realized Ashur had never gotten over her, and he would do everything in his power to get into her pants.

"Probably somewhere arguing or fucking. The animosity and sexual energy that comes from them could cause a building to explode."

"Well, they're about to get married. Isn't that the way it's supposed to be? Minus the animosity part."

"I wouldn't know. I guess we'll have to wait until next year and then I'll tell you."

I playfully nudged him with my shoulder. "You're so not funny."

"Yes, I am. Now let's mingle and then ditch this join..." Kevin trailed off, his eyes fixed on something, and then his jaw tightened.

"What?" I asked.

Across from us were Christopher Robinson and Katherine Franklin. They were another power couple in the Republican ranks. Chris and Kathy, as they were known in our social circles, were the go-to couple for donations and organizing fundraisers. If Kevin and I were the Barbie and Ken, then they were the Fred and Ginger. On top of their social perfection, they were a genuinely kind pair. Just like Kevin and me, they were expected to announce their engagement any moment.

"Am I missing something? Chris and Kathy are great. If only everyone in our party were like them, we wouldn't have such a bad reputation."

Kevin ignored me and continued to watch the couple. Kathy was showing off her engagement ring, and then I noticed Chris stare in our direction. There was a deep sadness that touched his eyes a second before his attention turned back to Kathy.

That was when I realized who Chris was to Kevin.

"Oh God, Kev. I'm so sorry." I twisted around and cupped his face. "Look at me."

He moved his gaze to mine.

"We'll get through this."

He nodded and then said, "I need a drink. Actually, I believe I want to get drunk."

He walked toward the bar with me following closely behind him.

THREE HOURS LATER, I SEARCHED THE HALLWAYS OF the museum to find Kevin. He'd kept it together for about twenty minutes but left the room when the emcee announced the news of Chris and Kathy's engagement. I wanted to go after him, but I had to keep calm and pretend all was great in my world. Then, when I thought I could escape to search for Kevin, I was cornered by donors and other politicians wanting my opinion on issues they favored. By the time I made it to the back of the room, Oscar had sent a text saying it was imperative to get Kevin out of the building. He must have seen Kevin drunk somewhere in the museum.

Thankfully, no one noticed I'd spent most of the evening alone. Well, no one except Veer, who'd lifted a brow with an unsaid question about Kevin when our eyes had caught for a moment. I'd ignored him, not wanting to stir up more emotions than I already felt. That brief second of communication showed me how connected we were, and my heart ached.

I couldn't let myself go down that particular rabbit hole or I'd end up in the same state as Kevin.

I glanced into a section with rows of antique documents and found it empty.

God, I hoped he wasn't in some corner drunk or passed out. There was no way I'd be able to sneak him through the building without causing a scene. Everyone would recognize him on the spot.

As I turned a corner, I came to an abrupt halt. Ashur and Tara held a very drunk Kevin up by the arms. His clothes were a rumpled mess, and his head was flopping back and forth.

"Oh fuck." I ran in their direction.

The moment Ashur saw me, he said, "We need to get you two out of here."

"Yes, but how?" I looked around, hoping no one would notice a presidential candidate holding his drunk friend.

Tara adjusted Kevin's weight on her shoulders. "God, what does he eat?"

"Let me." I took her place. "You're a good five inches shorter than me. It'll be easier for me."

She nodded. "I've called our security. They have a car waiting to take you home."

"Want to tell me what triggered this?" Ashur asked. "Since we came back from our last tour, Kevin rarely, if ever, gets drunk."

"It's not my place to say." I kissed Kevin's cheek. "Oh Kev, why did you ditch me? We could have left and gotten drunk at my house."

Ashur studied me. "You do care for him."

I frowned. "What the fuck does that mean?"

"You know exactly what I mean."

Tara stepped forward. "What Ashur is failing to say is that he is glad you and Kevin care so deeply for each other. And he's happy Kevin has you to lean on. Isn't that right, Ashur?"

"No."

"Ashur, I swear you could drive a woman to drink. How the hell am I going to help you win this damn election if you can't lie worth shit? You're a politician, for Christ's sake."

I sighed and shifted, trying to adjust Kevin's deadweight.

"Ashur, I love Veer, but we don't have a future. You have no idea how much I wish things were different." I pushed Kevin's hair from his brow. "What Kevin and I have is special. He is my friend, and I love him, but it's different. You should know as well as I do that one can marry someone they love but aren't in love with."

"Touché," Ashur said as he watched Tara.

Ashur could make Tara believe it was a business deal all he wanted. I knew the truth. I'd heard him say it. He wanted her and had found a way to get her. Hopefully, they wouldn't kill each other in the process.

A group of security personnel arrived, including Oscar and his team. They took an unconscious Kevin from us and carried him through a back hallway.

"Where do you want them to take you?" Tara asked as she typed on her phone.

"My townhouse. It has a private entrance and attached garage. No one can see Kevin like this." I took a step, then turned back and hugged Ashur. "Thank you."

"We're still family, Jaci. You've been my sister since the moment you and Sam got into your first scheme together." His voice grew gruff as he held me. "At the end of all of this, you can't forget that none of this means anything without the people you love."

"You do your damnedest to make the world think you're an asshole, but deep down you're all mush."

"If you say so," he grumbled, and hugged me one last time.

I kissed his cheek then moved to Tara. "I'm not sure when I'll see you again."

A slight gleam touched her eyes. "I believe it will be sooner rather than later." She leaned in and then whispered, "Expect a certain someone to name her pet project tomorrow."

I had completely forgotten the first lady was due to announce her support for the No Bride Initiative. What I hadn't expected was for the declaration to come so quickly. But now that I thought about it, it made sense. Tara was part of the campaign challenging the president. This was the best opportunity for Mrs. Edgar to strike.

I nodded and moved toward the exit.

CHAPTER THIRTEEN

"WHERE SHOULD I SET HIM, SENATOR?" one of my security team, Luke, asked me an hour later.

I gestured to the couch in the living room. "Lay Kevin there. Thank you."

The drive back home had been dismal at best. Watching a man who rarely, if ever, drank more than two glasses of anything get wasted because of another person made my heart ache. For years, I'd known about Kevin's lover, even if I hadn't known his identity. They'd met in college but kept their relationship quiet because of their conservative and affluent families.

Now that I knew it was Chris, all the secrecy made sense. No one would ever have suspected two of the most desirable men in the Republican Party were a couple, especially since both of them were in very public relationships with women.

I wondered if Kathy knew the truth. No, that wasn't

possible. She was one of those people so naive and kind that you wanted to keep anything that would upset her hidden. Plus, the way she'd showed off her ring made me think she believed her marriage to Chris would be real.

Poor Kathy. I hated to think of the devastation she would feel when she learned the truth.

God, this whole situation was a fucked-up mess.

Poor Kevin. Politics, religion, and family had forced him to live a lie. I guessed it was the reason we were perfect for each other.

If only I could take the heartache away from him. Would I feel this way the day I learned that Veer was getting married?

More than likely, yes. If the thought of it shredded something inside me, then the actual event would probably cause me to have the same reaction Kevin had, or worse.

I walked over to Kevin and brushed his hair.

"Is there anything else we can do for you?" Luke asked.

"No. I appreciate your help."

Luke nodded and left me with Kevin.

I sat down, kicking off my shoes. "Kev." I touched his cheek and then felt his forehead. "You need to wake up."

There was no response. He was out cold. I reached over for a blanket in a basket next to the sofa and tucked it around Kevin. The weather was still chilly in DC, and I wanted him to be warm.

I waited a few minutes, watching him, and then decided I had to get out of my ball gown. But first I'd better make sure everything was ready in case Kevin woke. After setting a trash can within easy reach for Kevin, I made my way down to the kitchen. A shadow was outside my back door, making me jump for a second before I realized it was another team of security. They took their job seriously and would never let anything leak about tonight. Hell, they'd kept a tight lid on my relationship with Veer, and we'd spent most of our days naked whenever he came to visit.

I made a pot of coffee and then poured two mugs. Walking over to the back door, I opened it and handed the cups to the guards. They both smiled and then went back to watching the perimeter.

I wondered what it would be like to live a life where privacy wasn't a luxury. Even when Samina and I were at Stanford, we had a personal detail. After all, I was the daughter of a United States senator, and Sam was the daughter of a technology billionaire.

I'd always wondered why our security detail hadn't ratted us out when we got into our antics. Even the one time when I'd had Devin and Ashur come from Texas and Louisiana to help us because we decided it would be fun to challenge a group of much older law students to a drinking challenge, which then ended up causing a bar brawl, the guards hadn't said a word to anyone. They'd just made sure we were protected and helped us escape the chaos we'd started. Too bad someone had taken a picture of us, and we'd gotten caught. But thankfully, Ashur with his tech knowledge—i.e. hacking skills—had been able to wipe any trace of the incident from the record.

It wasn't one of my better ideas, but what could anyone

expect? Sam and I had started law school at eighteen and had never experienced true college life.

Picking up a few water bottles and some pain meds, I returned to the living room to check on Kevin. He was still sleeping and hadn't moved a muscle. I set the water and the medicine on the side table and turned off the light before heading upstairs to my bedroom.

As I climbed to the first landing, something glinted in a decorative red glass bowl sitting on an inset shelf. It was Veer's favorite pair of Deakin & Francis cufflinks in a skull-and-crossbones design. I used to get so annoyed when he'd wear them. I'd tell him it wasn't appropriate attire for the governor of Texas, but he couldn't care less and would make sure to don them on every formal occasion to annoy me. After a while, his rebel edge became one of his more endearing characteristics. It was his way of saying nothing could tame him.

I picked up the heavy silver and gold pieces, and a wave of sadness engulfed me. I remembered how rushed we were to get out of our clothes that last night we'd spent together in this house. We hadn't seen each other for weeks, and the desperate need that seemed to pulse between us had been at an all-time high. We'd never made it up the stairs. Instead, I'd pushed him to the floor of the curved landing and rode him to a mind-blowing climax.

My nipples pebbled as I thought of a gloriously naked Veer letting me have my wicked way with him.

Shit. I had to snap out of it. This was not the time to fantasize about my ex. I had my soon-to-be fiancé passed out in my living room because his lover had decided to marry someone else.

God, that sounded so messed up.

Shaking my head, I reached for the hidden zipper on the back of my dress and made my way to my bedroom. A set of suitcases sat in the corner of the room, reminding me I had a four-hour drive ahead of me. A lonely four-hour drive, to be exact. There was no way in hell Kevin was going to be able to make it, and I had to attend the bipartisan gala in New York City. It was one of the few events where all the candidates running for office, including the president, would attend. Too bad I'd have to sit with the doofus and our fellow party colleagues. I smiled, thinking about how Dad had referred to President Edgar.

Slipping my dress off, I laid it on the back of an armchair and decided a few hours' sleep was in order. Instead of heading to the bathroom and taking off my makeup, I crawled into my bed, set my alarm, and shut my eyes.

I WOKE TO THE BLARING SOUND OF MY CLOCK.

I moaned. Five a.m. already. I'd barely had a few hours.

Smacking the evil device to silence, I rubbed the grit from my eyes and rolled out from under my covers.

I should check on Kevin. But first, I had to freshen up and feel semi-human at this ungodly hour of the morning.

Twenty minutes later, after a hot shower, I dressed in a pair of comfortable travel pants and a loose-ribbed sweater and then readied my briefcase for my road trip with plenty of work to keep me busy.

I sighed. I'd hoped to have a fun and relaxing weekend with Kevin, but now it was shot.

Making my way downstairs, I went to check on him.

He was stirring but still out of it.

Crouching in front of him, I set my hand on his chest. "Hey, handsome. You think you'll be okay here? I have to go."

He opened his heavy lids and moaned. "What the fuck did I do?"

"You got shit faced."

He groaned again and shifted to his side. "Jaci?"

"Yes."

"People like us don't get our happily ever after, do we?"

My lips trembled. "No, not in the traditional sense."

"You know what hurts the most?" He sat up and grabbed a water bottle, opened it, and then took a sip. "He never even considered being open, and I was stupid enough to hope he'd change his mind. It's like you and V. Doomed from the start. There was never a future, but you jumped in headfirst."

"Hey, you can't help who you fall in love with."

"Tell that to my mother, or half of our party. They think it is a choice."

"Kev, why haven't you ever told Ashur or Veer? They're your closest friends."

"You're my closest friend," he countered.

I frowned and quirked a brow.

"Because it's just not something we have ever discussed. Unlike women, most guys don't spill their deepest, darkest secrets to their friends."

"Well, you told me."

"That's because whenever I'm around you, I get verbal diarrhea."

"Whatever." I crossed my arms and tried to look stern but failed by smirking.

"And the fact that we're playing a game that requires full disclosure." He reached for the medicine bottle. "Hand me a pill, will you? My head hurts like a motherfucker."

I opened the bottled and dispensed three tablets into his palm. At that moment, my phone beeped, telling me it was time to go.

"Hey, I'm running late. Oscar is waiting to take me to New York."

"Stop worrying about me." He took his meds and relaxed back onto the couch cushions. "I'm not going to do anything stupid. I think I reached my limit last night. I'm sorry I'm bailing yet again on another weekend with you."

"I'll be sure to find some way for you to make it up to me."

"I have no doubt."

"Get some rest. You can stay the weekend if you want."

"I may do that. I need to wallow a little before I'm ready to face the world again."

I squeezed Kevin's hand and stood, picking up my shoulder bag.

"See you later, alligator," I said as I walked to the door.

Kevin laughed and responded, "After a while, crocodile."

CHAPTER FOURTEEN

FIVE MINUTES AFTER LEAVING KEVIN, I climbed into the limo, ready to get some work done, and came to an abrupt halt. Veer sat in the back, out of the sight of any camera's lens. He sipped his scotch and watched me.

The privacy glass of the limo was up, telling me Oscar knew Veer was in the back.

Veer had loosened his tie and had thrown his jacket on the seat next to him. He no longer looked the polished vice-presidential hopeful, but the sexy-as-sin man I'd fallen in love with and could no longer touch.

I waited for the door to close and the car to begin moving before I asked, "What are you doing here?"

He said nothing and stared at me, causing my heartbeat to accelerate. Just being in a small space with him made my skin tingle and body ache.

"How did you know Kevin wasn't going to be with me?"

"Ashur told me what happened. I doubt Kevin would be up for a long drive, so I thought I'd give you some company."

"You do realize it's a four-hour drive to New York," I said, trying to keep the desire from my voice and failing miserably.

A slight curve touched his lips, and I licked mine.

"We're going to the same fundraiser. It's more fuel efficient if we carpool."

I shifted, kicking off my shoes, about to step into a tumultuous pond I shouldn't even consider entering. "Is that right?"

"Absolutely." He set his drink in the holder next to him. "Now, I have four words for you."

I swallowed and said, "And what are they?"

"Take off your clothes."

My eyes immediately went to the bulge in his pants, which he adjusted to emphasize the length of his beautiful cock.

"I thought we broke up." I moved toward him, ready to assuage the desire I always felt for him. I was a glutton for punishment who was about to do something that would make things harder in the long run. But I couldn't help it. I needed him, and he was making it convenient for me to have him.

"It's for the best." He grabbed my arm when I was within reach and pulled me toward him.

I ended up sprawled against him. I held on to his shoulders as he parted my thighs and then settled my cleft along his hard, pulsing cock. A moan escaped my lips, and I rolled my hips to alleviate the throbbing that had flared to fire in my core.

"This is going to complicate things."

He threaded his fingers through my hair and tugged my head back. "Nothing has ever been simple between us. Why start now?" He rubbed the stubble of his beard along my jaw and neck. "I need you, Jaci. You're the only woman I've lost myself inside for the past three years. The thought of anyone else repulses me."

My heart clenched at his words.

"Veer. Don't say these things. It's hard enough as it is."

"What? Not tell you that whether we're together or not, I don't want another woman. That everywhere I go, all I do is think of you, even though I know you are going to marry one of my closest friends for the sake of both your careers."

"Yes. It hurts too much to hear it." I gazed into his hazel eyes. "I can't handle thinking this is anything more than a release of sexual need."

A muscle in his neck twitched, and he released his hold on my hair. "Is that how you want to do this, Jaci?"

Of course, it wasn't. I wanted Veer and the life I'd set myself up to achieve, but having both wasn't in the cards for me.

"Yes," I lied. "It can't be anything more."

I ran my fingers over the scar running the length of his right cheek and cupped the back of his neck, pulling him toward my lips and kissing him.

"So be it." He deepened our embrace, tongues dueling and savoring each other's taste.

His hands went to the hem of my sweater and then slid underneath to cup my breasts. He rolled my nipples through the fabric of my bra, creating a delicious sensation that tingled throughout my body.

"Are you wet, baby?" he murmured. "Does your pussy need my cock?"

"Of course, I need you. It's been six weeks. I think this is the longest we've gone without fucking in three years."

"Then show me how much you want it. Get on your knees and make him nice and wet for your soft, delicious pussy."

I slid off his lap, kneeling between his spread legs. I shimmied out of my pants and pulled my sweater over my head, leaving me in my bra and underwear.

"I want you naked. Take it all off."

Reaching behind me, I unclasped the hook of my bra and let the silky material drop to the floorboard of the limo.

As I reached for my thong, he said, "No. I've changed my mind. Leave it on. You are sexy as hell in lace. Especially lace that I bought you."

I leaned over, unbuttoning his tuxedo pants and carefully opening his fly to keep from catching his beautiful hard cock.

He helped me pull him out, letting his flared head hit my lips. I licked the pre-cum dripping along the slit and moaned, loving the clean, intoxicating taste of him. My tongue followed the thick vein running the underside of his thick cock, causing it to jump. Gripping the base, I engulfed him in my mouth, letting his hum of pleasure fill my ears as I took him almost to the base of his long length. As I came up, I followed the path with the squeeze of my palm.

"Oh Jaci. God, Jaci. That's it. Take me, baby."

I sucked him with long, slow pulls, knowing that was the way he enjoyed the movement of my mouth. The heat of his smooth, hot skin against my tongue sent a shiver down my spine.

I loved the feel of him, the taste of him, the essence of him. I bobbed up and down with my hands in tandem. His breath began to come in short pants, and his thighs quivered. He was close.

My hardened nipples ached and puckered tighter as I worked his cock. His arousal spurred mine. A low growl formed in the back of his throat. On a downward stroke, I rubbed the delicate spot behind his balls, causing a spasm to ripple through his thick, hard cock.

Preparing myself for the shot of his release deep in my throat, I swallowed.

"Oh no, you don't." He lifted me off the floorboard and pushed me back against the leather of the seat. His dripping length bobbed between us. "I don't come unless you come first. That's how it's always been, and that's how it will stay."

I whimpered. My own need dripped past my thong and onto the insides of my thighs. "Then make me come."

"You're very bossy, Senator Camden." He unbuttoned

his shirt, throwing it to the side, and then pushed his pants the remainder of the way down.

I reached out to run my fingers down his washboard abs. His body was a thing of fantasies.

"Veer," I moaned.

"Tell me what you want, and I may consider giving it to you."

"If you don't fuck me soon, I'm going to lose my mind."

"Now we can't have that." He spread my legs, ripped my underwear from my body, and positioned his cock at my entrance.

He pushed between the folds of my cleft, causing my back to bow and my pussy to clamp down on him.

"Oh God, you feel so good."

My body quickened after a few thrusts, and without warning, my core detonated. I clenched my eyes shut as my pussy flooded around Veer's pistoning cock.

"That's it, love. There's nothing like seeing your pleasure."

I rode out my orgasm, holding on to the leather seat I lay on. Before I could come down, I was climbing again, but this time there was a fierce edge to his thrusts.

"Do you make yourself come when you're alone, Jaci?"

I stared into his eyes. He loved watching me masturbate. It was one of those things that turned him on so much that he'd fuck me for an hour afterward.

"Yes."

"Who do you think of when your fingers are deep

inside your pussy, pressing against that special spot?" He rotated his hips, hitting the exact place he mentioned.

The pulsing inside me grew to steady contractions.

"You know very well it's you."

A smile touched his lips then a determined gleam entered his gaze as he altered his pace.

"Then why aren't we together?"

"You're the one who broke up with me." I pushed my heels against the seat, trying to match Veer's rhythm. "To become the vice-presidential candidate."

"What choice did I have? The woman I love would lose the chance at a dream she's had since she was a child. Plus, she's made a promise to marry another man."

"That's not fair."

"Fuck fair. What I want to know is, are you going to imagine me when you have to fuck Kevin? Because he'll have to blow his load on you if you want that precious dynasty you plan to create."

I wanted to cringe at his coarse words, his raw pain, but the sensation of his cock pounding into me left me no option except to feel the hard pull of our mutual need.

"Veer, not now. Don't say that when we're together. Please." I gripped his shoulders, digging my nails into his skin. "Kevin and I don't have that kind of relationship, and you know it. He's my friend, nothing more."

"Why?" He pulled out and slammed back in. "He is the Ken to your fucking Barbie. Isn't that what the media call the two of you? The ideal Republican package."

"Because," I gasped as another orgasm pulsed to life inside my core. "Oh God. I'm coming."

But all of a sudden, he pulled out.

"No," I screamed. "Don't leave me like this." I gasped for air, angry he would keep me hanging.

"You don't get to come yet. I want to know why." He rimmed the hard, angry head of his cock around the entrance of my pussy and then rubbed it back and forth through my slick cleft.

I blew out a frustrated breath and pushed back the hair that had fallen over my face.

"What does it matter?" Tears streamed down my cheeks.

"Because I want to know why Kevin doesn't do it for you? I want to know why you think of me but are going to marry him?"

"Because you're the only man I've ever loved." Tears came as if a faucet opened. "The only one I'll ever love."

He slammed back into me.

"And?" he gritted out.

"And because I made a promise."

"What is this promise that makes you two as thick as thieves?"

"Please, Veer," I sobbed. "I can't tell you."

"Is it that important?"

"Yes," I gasped. "I won't betray him, even for you."

Veer stopped his thrusts and gazed down at me. His breath was ragged, and sweat dripped down the sides of his temples. All of a sudden, something changed in his hazel eyes.

"Oh fuck. I know why." He sat up, pulling me with him while keeping his throbbing cock inside me. "God, why hadn't I thought of it before? That's why he got drunk last night after he heard the emcee announce Chris and Kathy's engagement. It wasn't because of Kathy, as I'd thought, but because of Chris. They've been friends since college. Kevin's..."

"No." I placed my hand over his mouth. "I don't want to discuss it. He's dealing with enough."

Veer cupped my face. "Okay. I understand now."

"Don't say anything to anyone." My lips trembled.

"I promise."

I swallowed and nodded. Veer's word was gold, and I knew Kevin's secrets were safe.

He drew me toward him, kissing me in the way I could never stop craving. I held on to his thick, muscular arms as I lost myself against his lips. Veer's cock twitched inside me, and my core quickened.

He pulled back and said, "I still hate this, but I get it. You and Kevin made this pact before I was in the picture. I wish..."

"Please, Veer. I don't want to think about it."

Veer sighed, releasing a resigned breath, and then lifted my hips.

As he slid me down his length, he whispered against my mouth, "Nothing matters outside of this limo for the next few hours. I want to enjoy every minute we have left."

"Yes," I gasped.

He repeated the motion a few times, bringing my arousal back in full force. My nipples ached, and my pussy flooded with desire.

I gripped the back of the seat, digging my nails in deep and taking over. I rose onto my knees and slammed down on his hard, hot cock.

"Oh fuck. Jaci." His hands flexed on my hips, but he let me command the rhythm.

My core rippled and then contracted. "Veer. I'm going to..." The words died on my tongue as my orgasm ripped through me.

I squeezed the thick root of his erection, and my body filled with a sensation I'd only experienced with this man.

I arched back, nearly losing my balance, but Veer caught me, bringing me flush against his chest as he spread my thighs, taking back control.

He pummeled my sex, drawing out my free-falling cascade.

"That's it, baby. Let go. This is us." His breath hissed out as his own orgasm loomed.

He swelled inside me and began to come, pumping hot jets inside me.

"Jaci," he called out.

His pleasure triggered another release, making my mind cloud.

After a few minutes, my body relaxed, no longer spasming around Veer's length. I listened to his heartbeat, pressing my face into his sweat-dampened chest and longing to say, "I love you." But I kept those words tightly inside. They would only cause us more pain.

What Veer and I had could never be public. And thinking about how my party would view our relationship if anyone found out made my stomach turn. No matter what I'd said before. Deep down, I knew this would be the last time we'd be together. Too much was at stake for both of us.

The best thing to do was to tell him now, but instead I closed my eyes and burrowed into the man who would hold my heart forever.

⁂

As the car pulled up to a private drive a few miles from his downtown hotel, I braced myself for a farewell I wasn't ready to say.

Veer and I had spent the ride making love and talking about everything but what would happen when we reached New York City. It wasn't until about thirty minutes ago when our mood went from playful and intimate to melancholy. We'd dressed and straightened our appearance in silence and then held hands.

The door opened.

"Governor George, your car is waiting for you around the corner," Oscar said as he waited for Veer to step out.

Veer nodded and gave me one last look as he moved into the early morning light.

He began to walk away, when I said, "Veer, wait."

I slipped out behind him, grabbing his suit jacket.

He turned and pulled me into a hug. "I know, baby. You don't have to say it."

"I do, or I won't be able to move on." I looked up at his face, cupping it. "I won't ever be alone with you again. Kevin is my future. You were my what-if. We have to move on, Veer. Otherwise, it will destroy even the memory of what we had."

He remained quiet, staring at me, so I continued.

"I want you to know this before I go. No matter how I felt when I learned about the election, I want you and Ash to win. Our country needs someone like Ashur in the White House. But promise me one thing."

"What?"

"Don't hate me when I go up against you in four years and win."

A smile touched his lips, and he ran a thumb down my cheek. "I love you, Jacinta Camden. Don't ever change."

"I love you too." A sob escaped my mouth.

He kissed the top of my head and threaded his fingers through my hair as I cried against his chest.

After a few moments, Oscar cleared his throat.

"Senator, we have to get you to your condo."

Reluctantly, I stepped out of Veer's arms, wiping my face. With one last glance, I stepped into the limo and felt my heart shatter.

CHAPTER FIFTEEN

A LITTLE PAST SIX THIRTY, I arrived at Invictus, the grand hotel sponsoring tonight's benefit. It was one of Kevin's hotels and had a reputation for treating every guest, whether they were celebrities or not, as if they were the most exclusive guests. The hotel was booked out anywhere between six months to a year in advance. The experience of staying there was as sought after as visiting the most popular tourist attractions of the city that never sleeps.

Lucky for me, I was the owner's "girlfriend" and could have a room available to me whenever I wanted. Unlucky for me, the president, all the presidential hopefuls, and their running mates were staying there. This was the reason I'd decided to spend the weekend in the upper east side condo my family owned for our trips to NYC.

After leaving Veer and spending a good hour crying, I'd checked in on Kevin, who was recovering miserably from a hangover. I'd offered for him to fly up and lounge around in PJs with me, while we ate pints of double chocolate chunk ice cream, but he'd declined, telling me it was time to move on and he needed some alone time to get himself together.

He was right, and I'd spent the rest of the day accepting the fact that my ambition came with a price. What started worrying me was, would the price both Kevin and I had to pay end up making us resent each other? He deserved love as much as I did, and the only way to have the type of relationships we both wanted was to sneak around.

We'd known from the start our relationship was a politically orchestrated arrangement, but now that it was going to become official, my stomach hurt with the knowledge we'd live out our lives wrapped in a well-planned lie.

I released a deep breath and opened my compact to check my makeup one last time. My makeup was flawless, as was my updo. The only thing that gave away the turmoil inside was my eyes.

Anyone who knew me would see the sadness, especially Tyler, who was going to fill in for Kevin tonight. He'd flown in from Louisiana an hour earlier and had decided to meet me at the hotel. I was both excited to see him and dreading it. My twin had a way of knowing what was in my mind before anyone else. Hopefully, we wouldn't have to discuss my melancholy or fucked-up love life until after we got back to our family condo.

I returned my compact to my clutch and waited for Oscar to open the door. The second I stepped out into the cool spring air, Tyler greeted me.

"Hey, little sis."

I smiled and hugged him, letting the comfort of his arms engulf me. He must have sensed my sadness since he held on for a few seconds longer.

When I stepped out of his hold, I said, "You're only two minutes older than me."

He shrugged his shoulders. "I'm still older, and therefore you are the baby of the family."

"Whatever," I halfheartedly grumbled.

He offered me his elbow. "Time for the Camden twins to rock this joint."

I slipped my arm through his. "I doubt there will be any opportunities to dance on tables at this event. Remember we are two well-respected members of Congress."

"Who like a good party," he muttered as we walked toward the hotel entrance. "Do you miss being carefree without all the attention and watching every step you take? Sometimes I wish we could go back to the way it was."

"If you remember, I've never had the chance to party it up without a chaperone. Someone was always watching over me in undergrad and later in law school. Hell, at Stanford it was twice as bad. It was Sam's security along with mine."

"It's not my fault you turned out to be super nerd

extraordinaire and entered college at fourteen, while my ass was still in high school like a normal kid."

"Stop your whining. You did your own version of trailblazing. You're one of the youngest members of the House."

"True, but becoming a politician ruined my love life."

Tyler's last relationship had ended in an epic disaster. He'd learned a little too late that the woman who he was planning to marry wanted him for his influence and social standing, not the man underneath the affluent name. I couldn't stand the gold digger from the moment I met her —all she talked about were the people I knew and if I could get her an introduction. It had taken two years and walking in on her fucking the neighbor for Tyler to accept that she'd played him.

"You and me both."

Tyler and I posed for a few photos and then entered the hotel.

"Will you do me a favor tonight?" I asked.

"Sure."

"Don't leave my side unless it is absolutely necessary. I am too exhausted to handle any confrontations with anyone, and without a doubt there will be a few people who are ready to strike at my heels."

"I'll do my best. Once our first lady makes her speech, all hell is going to break loose, and we know who they're going to point the finger at."

"Me, of course." I adjusted my clutch and nodded to a

few passing congressmen. "Who decided it would be tonight? You or Tara?"

"Yours truly." Tyler gave me a devilish grin that made him look like a little boy who was getting into mischief. "Tonight's benefit is all about children, making it the perfect place to announce an initiative aimed at ending the child bride trade. Tara and Mrs. Edgar happened to agree with my assessment. Plus, today is the last bipartisan event all the candidates will attend before the campaigning begins."

I gripped Tyler's arm. "I don't want you to get the backlash. If Edgar comes after me, don't get in the way."

"You think I'm worried about what Edgar thinks of me? He knows how to play the game as well as anyone. Besides, he went after you in the most underhanded way. He used your attacker and his father to question your ethics. Everyone knows he was the one who set up Decker's press conference. I feel it's time for payback."

"Calm down, superhero. This isn't about me. I put the demons of Decker Junior to bed years ago." Well, for the most part. No one truly got over being assaulted. "This is about Tara and clearing her name."

"Yes, yes. I know."

"Ty?"

He glanced at me.

"Thank you. I can always count on you."

"You're welcome. Dad taught us that no matter the party line, we had to do the right thing. Besides, I'm one of the few people who know you the best, and once you join a

173

crusade, there is no stopping you. So, it's either jump on your train or get run over."

My lips trembled. No matter what I faced or if they agreed with me or not, my family always had my back.

Tyler stopped midstep, turned toward me, and then ran a thumb under my eye. "Jaci, are you okay? I can tell when you've been crying. What aren't you telling me? Did something happen with V?"

I hadn't told Tyler anything that had happened between Veer and me over the past few weeks. I'd thrown myself so hard into various congressional bills and the planning for No Bride that I was able to avoid discussing my relationships.

"You could say that."

At that moment, Ashur, Tara, and Veer entered the building with their security team. As they moved toward the ballroom, Tara winked at me, while Ashur inclined his head. It was when Veer held my gaze that my heart broke and I looked away.

"This morning, Veer and I officially closed the chapter on our relationship. There is no future for us."

Tyler waited until the area cleared of people before he kissed the top of my head. "I'm so sorry."

I hiccupped. Tyler was another of the few people who would never judge me and my fucked-up love life.

"I knew we would end sooner or later. Now that it's happened, I feel like I should have known better than to get involved with Veer from the beginning."

"It's too late for should-haves. All you can do is focus on Kevin and your future."

Tyler and I made our way to the ballroom.

"Can I say something to you before we put our politician hats back on?" Tyler asked. "And don't think of this as judging."

"Sure, shoot." I waited, not sure what was about to come out of his mouth.

"You know Kevin is one of my best friends and I hold him in the highest regard."

I nodded. "Yes. Where are you going with this?"

"What I don't understand is why are the two of you so determined to follow through on this pact you made almost ten years ago?"

"We have our reasons."

"I get that together you've created the image that will land you in the White House and that you care for each other. But you aren't in love. You both love different men. Don't you guys deserve to find authentic relationships?"

I stared at Tyler, not sure what to say. "You know?"

He frowned at me. "Of course, I damn well know. Kevin and I have been friends since college. I was the one who helped him keep his shit together the first time Chris broke up with him. Just like you keep your promises, I kept mine."

"You're okay with this?"

"Jaci, now you're just pissing me off."

I winced. "Sorry."

"I'm a conservative, but I'm not an asshole. Just like you, in some areas, I'm more progressive than others."

He held the scowl on his face, telling me I'd hurt his feelings. Out of the two of us, he was the more sensitive twin.

"I'm truly sorry. I should have known better."

The hardness left his face, and he said, "So are you going to answer my question?"

I thought for a moment. "If Kevin ever wanted out of this pact to find a different future, I wouldn't hesitate. But for me, all I can say is at least I had a short time to experience love."

"You are so hardheaded."

"That's why I make such a good politician."

We both laughed and moved toward our table.

"LADIES AND GENTLEMEN, I PRESENT THE FIRST LADY of the United States, Amanda Tyson Edgar."

After a large round of applause, Mrs. Edgar began her speech.

The anticipation bubbling inside me caused me to fidget with my hands under the table. Amanda Edgar was about to announce her pet project for the remainder of her tenure in the White House. No one would be expecting it, especially not her husband, who only seemed to be half listening to her words so far.

The man was in for a big surprise.

It was amazing how things had turned in the last few weeks. What had originally been a way to pay back President Edgar for her humiliation had turned into something the first lady wholeheartedly supported. She'd spent an extraordinary amount of time learning everything possible about Tara's efforts. I'd played the middleman with the help of Tyler's contacts and in doing so had found an initiative I could stand behind as well.

I glanced over at the table where Tara sat with Ashur and Veer. She caught my gaze and gave me an anxious smile. She was as nervous as I was. The first lady's statement would put Tara in the spotlight once again, but at least it would be in a positive light.

"Before I finish, I have a story to tell you." The first lady paused, taking a deep breath, and then scanned the room, lingering on her husband.

Goosebumps prickled my skin as I readied myself for the major fallout that would begin as soon as the speech ended.

"Recently, I was introduced to a young lady who has put her life on the line to save countless others. She is a crusader in the fight to stop the epidemic of human trafficking in the world. Over the last two months, her efforts have come under scrutiny due to her involvement in negotiations with men of questionable character for the freedom of American girls."

A murmur went through the crowd. Everyone knew Mrs. Edgar was talking about Tara.

"That's right, of the girls released from horrible futures

as child brides, seventy were American citizens. And because of this crusader for human rights, who I consider a friend, those children were freed and are now in safe homes. My friend is a hero, but she can't save children like these alone. Therefore, I have decided we will join forces in her efforts to stop the sale of young girls as child brides. As of today, I will become the director of the No Bride Initiative, an organization with the sole purpose of ending a long history of child enslavement through marriage.

"As a conservative, I value every single human life on our planet. I may not be able to affect change in the world as a whole, but I can in our great nation. With this said, I challenge all of you, no matter your party officiation, to join me in stopping the silent epidemic we should no longer ignore.

"Thank you and have a wonderful rest of the evening."

There was quiet for a few seconds before the first clap echoed, followed by another and then another, eventually leading to a standing ovation.

The first lady held her head high as she moved to take her place by the president. This was the moment she took the spotlight from her husband and came out from the shadows. No one would doubt she wasn't independent of the president again.

I hated to think what kind of explosion would happen in private between them. More than likely very heated, with Edgar doing most of the talking. In the end, I had no doubt Amanda Edgar would come out on top. The president may not realize it, but his wife just saved the legacy of his presidency by going against him.

"Checkmate," Tyler whispered.

I responded with, "Not quite. We still have a bumpy road ahead, but soon."

CHAPTER SIXTEEN

"Senator Camden, please follow me" were the first words I heard as I walked out of the ladies' lounge.

There was no mistaking the man who stood in front of me as anything other than Secret Service.

I'd expected a reprimand to come in the next few days, but it surprised me the president was willing to do it on the same night as his wife's announcement. For the last two hours, Edgar had played the supportive and proud husband.

I glanced toward Tyler who was deep in conversation with a Lousiana constiuant who was a donor. He motioned to come to me, but I shook my head. Tyler had to keep the big money people happy.

"Before I go anywhere, I will inform my team about my whereabouts."

The agent opened his mouth as if to argue, but then

decided against it when he saw Oscar and a few of his team approach.

"Senator, is there a problem?"

"No, everything is fine. It looks like the president would like to have a word. Would you mind telling Tyler where I am?"

Oscar glanced at a short, heavily built man. "I will accompany you."

"That won't be necessary," said the agent, giving Oscar a glare that would have had a lesser man shaking in his pants.

"As I said, I will accompany Senator Camden. Personal security is allowed as long as they have authorization. I have clearance at all levels." Oscar held the man's stare.

Oscar was former military and FBI who'd maintained all credentials when he'd moved into the private sector. If there was anyone who knew protocol, it was him.

After a few moments of scowling, the agent turned. "Follow me."

We were led to a bank of elevators and then to the third floor. I entered a private lounge where the president sat smoking a cigar.

"President Edgar, you asked to see me?"

He remained seated as he glowered at me. "You think you're so clever, don't you?"

"I don't follow," I said. It was better to pretend ignorance than admit anything.

"You got Amanda involved behind my back. Now if I

oppose anything Tara Zain does, it'll look like I'm against my wife. Zain is marrying one of my opponents, and because of you, my wife has all but aligned herself with them."

I stared him in the eyes, not giving him even a flicker of uncertainty. This plan was risky, but until this moment I hadn't realized how.

I knew without a doubt if I were a man, the current tactic of a private meeting to intimidate me would never have happened. I would have received a pissed-off phone call at most.

"I honestly have no idea to what you are referring. Mrs. Edgar's involvement in the No Bride Initiative has nothing to do with me."

"So, you're saying Amanda contacted Tara Zain on her own and had no assistance from you?"

"This is something you should ask her. Mrs. Edgar is an intelligent woman who sees the merits of what Tara Zain is trying to accomplish."

"I do not want my wife involved in some feminist crusade." He slammed his hand on the table next to him.

"Saving the lives of young girls is not a feminist crusade."

"Then what is it? Except a thorn in my side." He stood, coming toward me. "You will advise her to step down. Do I make myself clear?"

I lifted my chin. He thought towering over me would scare me. Men in politics had used this move too many times to affect me anymore.

"I will do no such thing. Besides, you need this as much as Mrs. Edgar does."

"Pray tell, young lady. Why do I need Tara Zain's project?"

"To save the negative legacy of your administration, of course. If the polls are accurate, then your approval rating is at an all-time low and in severe need of a boost if you want any chance of reelection."

I dared him to deny what I was saying. Instead, he laughed and patted me on the shoulder.

"Girl, I knew you were good, but this shows you can cut it with the big boys. Richard Camden is the best at behind-the-scenes negotiations. I'm glad he taught you well."

Was the condescending man trying to turn this into something he orchestrated to show my skills?

"I am not my father's puppet, nor yours."

The smile left his face. "I see."

"I believe it is time I returned to the benefit."

He grabbed my arm a second before I turned to leave. "You may think you won this round, but remember you need me to have any hope of making it to the White House. Don't ever fuck with me again or I'll make it impossible for you to run for any office ever again."

Oscar moved in my direction as did the Secret Service officers around the room.

I shook Edgar's hand off before things escalated into something neither of us could recover from. I knew Oscar wouldn't hesitate to put the president on his ass if he perceived him as a danger to me.

"Threats don't work on me, Mr. President. Your friend Decker tried this, and now he's lucky if anyone takes him seriously. Just because I'm a woman doesn't mean I'm weak. At this juncture of your presidency, you need me more than I need you."

"You're working to get Kumar elected. I see it now. Where is your party loyalty?"

"My political association does not mean I will follow blindly. For the record, I have nothing to do with the Kumar-George ticket, but if they won, I wouldn't be disappointed."

I walked out the door, followed closely by Oscar.

I kept my body from shaking until I reached the main hall of the hotel.

Holy shit, I'd just challenged the president and essentially told him to fuck himself.

What had come over me? I was supposed to continue to play the game.

I placed a hand over my stomach. Sooner rather than later I'd feel the wrath of tonight's confrontation. I hoped I was the only one affected by the fallout.

"Senator, why don't you take a few moments before you return to the ballroom?"

I nodded and took a seat on a bench positioned near a wall of glass overlooking a large garden and pond.

I rubbed my temples as I felt the first pangs of a migraine developing.

"Oscar, would you mind getting me a sparkling water?"

"Sure. Please don't go anywhere until I return." He gave me a stern look that said he thought I'd disappear if he wasn't around to keep an eye on me. I guess I deserved it since I tended to keep things from him.

"I promise. I'll stay right here."

For the next few minutes, I gazed at the beautiful play of lights against the rippling water on the other side of the glass. Once dinner was over, Tyler and I would make our exit and then spend the evening eating junk food and watching the lights of the city below us from our condo.

"Ahh, there she is—the party's darling."

All the hairs on the back of my neck stood up when I heard the voice I hadn't had to encounter in almost seven years.

I knew this day would come, but I hadn't expected it to be tonight.

"Go away, Grey, unless you want the police to arrest you for violating the restraining order I have against you." I kept the tremor out of my voice.

Shit, I thought I was over what he'd done to me, but with him standing behind me, the anxiety and fear surfaced as fresh as the day he'd cornered me in his family's estate. At least this time, there were security cameras to catch everything. And I knew with no doubt, Kevin would be the first one to help me leverage any tapes against Decker Junior.

"You think I'm afraid of you? You ruined my life."

I glanced at my phone, pretending disinterest. Hopefully, Oscar would get here soon. A tinge of sweat broke out on the back of my neck.

I had to stay calm.

"You can't ruin a life that wasn't remarkable in the first place."

Fuck, why had I said anything? I knew I shouldn't engage him.

To hell with it. The bastard would never have power over me again. I'd worked too hard for the past years to let him even get a hint of how uncomfortable I was feeling.

"I did you a favor. If it weren't for me, you'd never have gotten the balls to make it to Congress. You should be thanking me."

My temper flared, making me stand to face him, and the fear I'd had disappeared, replaced by ruthless anger. "You're an asshole. You tried to rape me. Do you have any idea what that does to a woman?"

"You're a drama queen." He rolled his eyes. "It's not like my dick gave you what your hoity toity ass was begging for."

The thought of his dick anywhere near me made me want to vomit.

"I suggest you leave, Grey. You have stayed past my limit for your presence. Besides, there are reporters hiding around every corner, and one of them is bound to hear you."

I glanced around and cringed inside. Of course, when I

wanted people to snoop into my interactions, there wasn't a single soul to be seen.

"Good. I hope they record this. I think they need to know what a conniving bitch you are. They'd agree that you asked for it. You kept it quiet because you wanted to hold it over our heads."

"Oh, come off it. The reason you can't get a job where you don't have to work is because you spend most of your days high or drunk."

"I'm not a drug addict." His face contorted to one of rage. "You and your family put that shit out to the public."

"You are as delusional as ever." That was the moment I noticed his appearance. His eyes were bloodshot, and he wasn't in a tux as the rest of tonight's gala attendees. He wore a rumpled navy button-down and jeans. He also reeked of alcohol.

Fuck, he was high. Why hadn't I seen this earlier? He'd had a similar look on his face when he'd cornered me years ago. I couldn't believe I'd just wasted the last few minutes of my life talking to a man who more than likely wouldn't remember anything he said or did.

"I'm not crazy. Stop looking at me like I'm a bug under a microscope." He moved toward me, making me retreat.

"Stay away from me. You're already violating the restraining order. Don't make it worse by getting arrested for assault."

"Might as well make it worth it." He advanced until my back hit the glass wall behind me.

I grimaced as he gripped my jaw in a painful hold. I tried to look around, but he tightened his hold on my face.

I dug my nails into the back of his hand, drawing blood. This fucker was going to learn I wasn't going to take his shit. I hadn't in the past and the hell if I would now.

"Get your fucking hands off her." Veer's face was a mask of fury as he strode toward us.

He grabbed Grey by the neck and slammed him against the wall.

"Don't ever touch her. I will kill you if you ever touch her again."

"What are you going to do, George? Someone is bound to see us. You lay one hand on me, and they will ruin your career. Forget about becoming vice president—you'll wind up in jail." Grey lifted his face. "Go ahead, hit me and see what happens."

"Your threats mean nothing to me. Just like all those women that you didn't care about when you put your hands on them, I don't care." Veer's grip on Grey's collar tightened.

I had to stop this.

"Veer," I said softly. "Look at me."

His gaze turned to me. "Jacinta, he would have raped you seven years ago if you hadn't broken his nose. Who knows how many women he's succeeded in assaulting? He would have hurt you tonight. He's garbage."

"Well, this garbage was about to have a dick in her cunt."

At that moment, Veer threw Grey to the floor, with him on top of Grey.

"You motherfucker. I will kill you for even thinking to lay a hand on her." Veer slammed his fist into Grey's jaw and then followed it with one to his abdomen. "You will never." Punch. "Hurt another." Punch. "Woman." Punch. "Ever again."

Oscar ran up to us, followed by a group of Secret Service agents. They jumped in, pulling Veer off Grey.

"Let me, goddammit. That bastard deserves to die. That piece of shit was hurting her."

My hands went to my aching cheeks and chin, knowing I would probably have bruises all over the lower half of my face by morning.

Veer caught my movement, and his eyes darkened with even more fury. He pulled free and charged toward Grey. "When I'm done with you, you'll wish you were dead."

The agents grabbed Veer, pulling him back again, but not before he landed three more punches to Grey's face.

I had to get Veer under control, or without a doubt, I knew he'd kill Grey. The rage in him was bubbling over. Veer was so calm that when his anger set free, it was almost impossible to hold him back.

I stepped in front of him and hoped he would listen.

"Veer. Let him go. He's not worth it. He can't hurt me anymore."

CHAPTER SEVENTEEN

"Let him go, Veer."

I cupped his face and then gripped his shoulder, hoping he would stop struggling against the hold Secret Service had on him and focus on me.

Veer's eyes never left Grey Decker's fallen form, but he wasn't trying to pull free of the agents.

"Please. For me. He's not worth it," I pled. "He can't hurt me anymore."

Veer clenched his jaw and then turned to me. "That piece of shit doesn't deserve to breathe the same air as you, or any woman, as a matter of fact."

"Let it go. He's not worth it," I repeated. "He doesn't deserve your hatred. That's giving him too much power."

He opened his mouth to argue, but I cut him off.

"Don't make me sing that song that makes Sam want to run for the hills. You know I will, and off-key on top of it."

"You wouldn't torture us like that." A slight smirk touched his lips.

"Try me." I ran my thumb over the swollen corner of his lip where Grey must have gotten in a jab.

The hard edge of his face softened.

The agents released their hold on Veer and moved to pick up Grey.

We stared at each other for a few seconds, as if we hadn't just been in the middle of a brawl with a politician's son or in the middle of a hallway of a hotel jam-packed with the political elite and the media.

This man had come to protect me. He wasn't mine, yet he'd been here. Veer stood up to the man who'd taken a piece of my younger years and completely obliterated the memories, replacing them with new ones.

Maybe it was the violence mixed with the adrenaline of the situation, but all I could think about was getting Veer naked, inspecting his glorious body for any bruises and then kissing them better.

A throat cleared. "Senator. I think it would be wise to take the Governor to straighten his appearance."

I scanned Veer's clothes. His tux was rumpled and stained with Grey's blood. His normal messy hair was a bit more tousled, giving him an even more sexy edge than usual.

"Thanks, Oscar." I glanced at him. "Can you do me a favor?"

"No need to ask. No one will know what transpired tonight." Oscar glanced at the Secret Service agents. "The hallways are currently empty and I will have my men sweep the area and the security feeds for anyone who could have seen the altercation."

"Don't worry, Senator," said the one who I assumed was the agent with the highest rank. "We are well aware of Mr. Decker's history. No one will know what happened tonight. You have our word." He then gestured to another man who threw Grey over his shoulder and took him away from us.

I wasn't sure how all the internal politics worked, but I had no choice but to accept them at their word. Besides, Oscar would do his best to protect my interests as he'd done since I was a teenager.

I offered Veer my hand. "Come with me."

His gaze had never left me since his focus had shifted from Grey to me. My pulse accelerated. He had to know what was going on inside me.

"Okay," was all he said and moved toward the hallway leading to the private elevators with me a step behind him. His security and another set of Secret Service agents followed us, and although I wanted to be alone with Veer, I knew it was for the best.

We'd ended our intimate relationship for good earlier today, and it would break the necessary distance if we were in a room without supervision.

As we entered the elevators, I moved to a back corner, and then Veer came to stand next to me. His finger grazed my hand, making my breath hitch. He glanced my way but said nothing.

He cupped the back of my neck, and as he brought his palm down, it settled on the hollow of my back. His slightest touch sent a flood of desire through my core, and the throb of need I felt whenever he was near came fully awake.

Shit, there was too much sexual tension floating between us.

I tried to sidestep but ended up pressed against the wall of the cab with Veer even closer to me. I looked down at my hands and caught the distinct bulge underneath the front seam of Veer's pants.

I almost cupped him, wanting to squeeze his long, hard length; instead I restrained myself and folded my arms.

Fuck, I was in serious trouble.

The agents in front of us shifted and gave each other looks. I cringed inside. They had to have sensed the tension behind them.

The moment the lift opened, they stepped out and directed us to Veer's suite.

"Governor, when you are ready to return let us know. We will remain outside."

They waited for us to enter and immediately shut the door. The room was nothing less than what I'd expect of a hotel owned by Kevin. It was over-the-top elegance without looking gaudy. The floor-to-ceiling windows gave a breathtaking view of Central Park and the city that never slept.

The interior was a mix of modern, clean lines and small touches that kept the room from looking industrial.

"I'll get you a drink." I moved to the bar cart near the wall of windows. My hands shook as I picked up a decanter and poured a rich amber liquid into a tumbler.

"Jaci," Veer crooned from behind me, and my heartbeat jumped. "Stop."

I paused, setting the decanter down. However, I refused to turn and look in his direction.

"Veer, we can't."

"Can't what, Jacinta?" He gripped my shoulder, and I closed my eyes.

Shit, shit, shit.

My cleft grew damp, and my clit began to swell, as did my breasts against the confines of my dress.

He'd made love to me at least four times on our drive to New York City, and still, I hadn't gotten him out of my system. With a few words, I was ready and willing for him.

"Turn around," he commanded, and without thought, I moved.

His eyes were molten gold and reflected the desire I felt.

We stood staring at each other for what felt like hours. Then in a frenzied shift, we reached for each other and our lips collided.

"Veer," I gasped as his tongue pushed past my lips.

I shoved his jacket off his shoulders and tugged his shirt free of his waistband. I tried to unfasten his buttons but got frustrated and yanked the shirt open, sending studs everywhere.

The second his upper body was bare, I threaded my fingers into his hair. Before I knew it, my back hit a wall.

He bunched my dress over my hips and pulled my legs to wrap around his waist. He kissed down my throat and his hands massaged my breast, causing a pained, guttural cry of need to escape my mouth.

My soaked pussy screamed for Veer, and I wasn't sure what to do to get him to forgo foreplay and fuck me.

"This is going to be hard and fast."

"Good." I dug my nails into his shoulders and moaned. "Stop talking and do it."

"Jaci, if you don't shut up and let me fuck you, your ass is going to glow bright red."

"Either way you screw my brains out, so it shouldn't matter."

A growl rumbled deep in his throat. "God, Jaci. Don't ever change."

He tilted away from me, keeping my thighs locked against him. His fingers found the crotch of my panties and then ripped them from my body.

The next thing I heard was the sound of his zipper echoing in the air and his hard cock pressing into my sopping cleft.

I arched against him at the exquisite feel of his thick, hard girth spreading my tight core.

"That bastard will never hurt you again. I will kill Decker before he gets close to you one more time."

I rotated my hips with his thrusts. "He doesn't have

any power over me. He is a weak man with no future. Don't let him take any piece of what we had."

"Have," he countered.

I wanted to agree, to say we'd find a solution, but I'd be lying. There was no way to have what we needed from each other and the goal we were both striving to achieve.

"No. There has always been truth between us no matter how much it hurt. I won't change it."

He closed his eyes and leaned his forehead against mine. "Jaci, I don't know how I'm going to do this without you."

He pulled out and slammed back in. I cried out in a pleasure-pain only he could ever make addictive. My breasts ached, and my nipples beaded to sharp peaks, pushing against the coarse fabric of my gown.

"You can do this like you've done everything—on your terms. You don't need me."

He gripped my hands and then captured them above my head. His face grew into hard lines as it had been when he was confronting Grey.

"I would give up everything if I knew I'd have you, but I know it won't ever happen."

I arched toward him and whispered against his lips, "Stop, Veer. Right now, it is only us. This is all I can give you. If things were different..." I trailed off.

Tears burned the back of my eyes. We should never have come up here. I knew better, and I'd done it anyway.

"Things will never be different. You love your career

more than me. Have always loved it more than me. I thought I could handle it. But I was wrong."

My heart ripped at the pain in his words.

He pulled out to the hilt and slammed balls-deep. "I need a woman who will love me enough to compromise, to make my dreams hers as I'd make her dreams mine."

"Veer, I'm begging you. Stop."

"Fine. I won't tell you what I wish. Instead I'll fuck you so hard that years from now you'll remember what you cast aside."

He set a pace that had me helpless against the need driving him. His hold on my wrists intensified as my core quickened to a desperate race for release.

"Come. Come for me. One last time."

My pussy spasmed and detonated around his pistoning cock. Each wave of ecstasy fed another until all that was left was the decadent pleasure he was bringing my body. I clenched my eyes tight and pressed my head against the wall.

"Your turn." I contracted my internal muscles and rolled my hips.

He smacked the side of my ass, and he came with hard, deep groans against my neck.

After a few minutes, my heartbeat calmed, and I kissed the side of his face. "We need to get back."

He lifted his head, revealing his beautiful hazel gaze filled with resounding sadness.

He stepped back, letting me slide to the ground and

pulling his softening cock free of my body. He tucked himself into his pants and continued to gaze at me.

The wetness of his cum slid down between my thighs, making the finality of our relationship painfully clear.

"I'm so sorry, Veer."

He took tissues from a box near him, crouched down, and wiped the remnants of our pleasure from my body.

Once he finished, he tugged my gown into place, rested his head on my stomach, and said, "This can never happen again. We won't ever be alone again."

"I know." I ran my fingers through his hair.

"I'll marry someone else."

I swallowed the jagged lump in my throat.

"I know."

He glanced up at me and then stood. "I'll always remain faithful to her, Jaci, no matter how I feel for you."

"I know. It's who you are."

He cupped my face and kissed my parched lips.

"Goodbye, Veer." I pulled out of his hold and walked to the door.

My hand shook as it covered the knob. I wanted so much to say fuck the consequences, to say I'd rather have Veer than my dreams.

How was I going to live without him?

I couldn't do this. I couldn't leave the only man I'd ever loved.

I began to turn, but Veer spoke, "No, Jaci. Don't say it. If you do, I'll never let you go. It wasn't fair, what I said.

You have to do this. If not for you, then do it for me. I don't ever want you to have any regrets."

"Veer," I hiccupped, still holding the doorknob as tears streamed down my face. He was right. I would wonder what life could have been if I never tried for the White House.

"Go, baby."

I nodded, and before I lost my nerve to keep from making a commitment that had the potential to destroy us, I stepped into the hallway. I wiped my wet eyes with the back of my hands and walked toward the elevators, closing the most precious chapter of my life.

CHAPTER EIGHTEEN

I WALKED into my Capitol Hill office to a frenzy of activity. My staffers, Kimberly, Frank, and Terry, were running around and giving each other directions, and Tracy had a frazzled expression on her face as she held two phones on her shoulders.

"What happened in the time I was out?" I asked Kimberly, glancing at my watch. "I've only been gone for an hour and a half."

Before she could answer, the office phone rang.

"Answer it then tell me."

She picked up the receiver and then gestured to Frank for a pen.

Whatever was going on, I had a feeling I would be spending the night at the office.

Since the eventful night in New York City three weeks ago, the election campaign had jumped into full swing as did the president's efforts to pass various bills, and then a few days ago, Kevin and I had announced our engagement. This meant I had little or no time to myself.

With the exception of random dinners with Kevin, most of my days were spent either in meetings surrounded by people jockeying to secure my vote or helping Mrs. Edgar and Tara with the No Bride Initiative, which had garnered such backing across party lines that the president had no choice except to support the efforts.

I was still waiting for the fallout on that one. I wasn't naive enough to think I'd gotten off scot free. Edgar had a reputation for holding grudges, and sooner or later, there would be repercussions.

Tracy hung up her phone and looked at me. "Senator, we have a major problem. I suggest you check your cell."

I set my shoulder bag on a nearby sofa and pulled out my mobile. When I opened my news app, I found at least four major news agencies reporting about the secret relationship between vice-presidential candidate and Texas Governor Veer George and Texas Senator Jacinta Camden. Articles were questioning my loyalty to the party and others calling for an investigation into the illicit affair between two high-level Texas state officials.

The article that ignited a migraine was one where a reporter asked the president about the breaking news. He'd laughed while standing next to Grey Decker on a golf course and said, "Nothing stays hidden in politics, especially our bedfellows. Well, one thing can be said, for a supposed conservative, she has poor taste in men. But what can be expected when her best friend is a liberal?" And then he posed for pictures.

He couldn't leave it at Veer and me but had to throw Samina in the mix.

"Oh fuck." I pinched the bridge of my nose. "When did this hit the air?"

"A few minutes ago," Terry answered. "However, we started a media lockdown about half an hour ago when I received a call from my friend at *The Washington Post* to give us a heads-up."

"Tell them thank you."

She nodded.

I had hired Terry not only for her killer resume but her ability to make friends with the most unlikely people. She had a way of garnering loyalty, and I'd known it would be foolish not to have her on my team.

"Has anyone contacted my family or Kevin? We need to prepare them."

Tracy set a glass of water and a bottle of my migraine medicine in front of me and said, "I called Representative Camden right after the call from *The Post*. You were in a secured session, so there wasn't a way for us to contact you without causing unnecessary attention. Mr. Stanton agrees with our media blackout and will remain in Texas on his family's ranch to keep any undue attention away from you."

Boy, did I owe Kevin for his volunteer sequestering at his estate. It probably would force him to take a break from the nonstop traveling he'd done over the last few weeks. He loved the outdoors, and the 70,000-acre estate he owned in West Texas would give him the perfect excuse to spend some time doing what he loved, hunting and sleeping under the stars.

I opened the container, tapped out a tiny white pill, and then drank down the yucky-tasting meds with the cool water.

Frank came around his desk and offered me an envelope. "This is some data I was able to gather."

Frank was probably the best analyst anyone could find. He could weed out the tiniest details within minutes of an event occurring. Samina had recommended him to me after I'd won the election. She, in all honesty, had poached him from her father's technology company with a promise of a future where he would get to show off his skills and not be stuck in a cubicle all day.

"What about Dad?" I asked as I opened it.

"Your father is on his way to Louisiana. I have someone waiting at the airport to get him updated as soon as he lands," Kimberly said as she hung up the phone. "I've also arranged for a return flight back to DC for him. Senator Camden isn't one to sit back when anyone attacks the ones he loves."

A vein pulsed on Kimberly's forehead. She was the first lady's niece and had a serious dislike for her uncle ever since his long-term affair with an assistant was revealed to the public.

"I appreciate you taking care of this." I pulled out the contents of the envelope and groaned.

Image after image of Veer and me appeared. Some were from social gatherings, without anything salacious, but there were a few that made me cringe. There was one from the last weekend Veer and I had spent at my house in Austin with our friends. I was only wearing Veer's shirt and was sitting on his lap. There was no doubt we were lovers.

And then there were two pictures of the morning after the drive from DC. Veer was holding me close as we said our goodbyes. Tears streamed down my cheeks, and both our faces couldn't hide the love we felt for each other or the shadows of sadness.

My heart ached at the memory. I'd spent so many days pushing back the pain and loneliness, but now seeing the pictures, I could no longer pretend I was okay.

This was a private moment between two people whose hearts were breaking, and a fucking reporter had followed us to get the picture. At least this time, they hadn't doctored them or made me look like a drunken whore as Decker had tried to do seven years ago.

I looked at the people in the room. The looks in their eyes told me they'd all seen what Frank had put together.

"You did nothing wrong, Senator," Kimberly whispered. "You need to keep your head high and not feed into the media spectacle."

"The world won't see it that way. After all, I'm engaged to one man while having an affair with another."

"None of the pictures show when or where this

happened. For all anyone knows, it could have been years ago," Trisha added.

I gave her a tight smile and then turned to Kimberly. "Send a message to your aunt and tell her it won't be a good idea to meet today."

"I'll text her now. Aunt Amanda will understand."

"If I may add something, Senator?"

I turned my attention to Frank again.

"Every one of those pictures was taken before the first lady announced her involvement with the No Bride Initiative. I have no doubt President Edgar is involved." He paused.

"But..." I probed, resting my hand on the back of a nearby chair.

"...but the one who had you followed was Grey Decker Senior. He blames his tarnished career on you and Senator Kumar-Camden, he blames you for his son's drug habit, and he blames you for the fact he is under investigation in Texas."

I nodded. "You're right. Decker Senior is the reason the photos of my lunch with Tara and Sam were leaked to the press two months ago and most logically the reason these images were available for the media now."

"Plus," Tracy interjected, "the Deckers are spending more time with the president than usual. If you noticed, anytime a rally or event happens, one of the Deckers is present. This was not the case during the last election."

I clenched my jaw. "The bastards have been planning something against me for a while. Why else were the pictures ready for distribution while they were enjoying an afternoon together on the golf course? This was Edgar's way of trying to put me in my place."

"*Trying* is the operative word." Kim smiled. "I think it's time to call in some favors, Senator."

My lips turned up at the corners. I could handle anything these guys threw at me. "I couldn't agree more."

My phone buzzed. Glancing down, I saw it was a message from Tyler saying he was on his way up with Sam. Immediately, my confidence from seconds earlier faded. I could keep the cool, always-in-control image up with everyone except Tyler and Sam. They'd see right through me.

Releasing a deep breath, I moved toward my office. "If you'll excuse me. I need to gather my thoughts and make a few calls. Keep the media lockdown going, and once I talk to my advisers and my family, we'll implement a plan on how to handle this."

No one said anything, but I felt the weight of their gazes.

As I entered my office, I let the door shut behind me and collapsed onto my chair.

I hated Edgar with every ounce of my being. He wanted to pay me back for flouting his authority. He was determined to humiliate me, to make me look like a whore, to ruin my reputation.

I guessed this was the price a woman paid for entering the political game. The fucker had a full-blown affair as a married man, but he was pretending he was morally superior. I couldn't understand how he could stand next to Grey Decker, a man who was currently under investigation for harassing and manipulating anyone who got in the way of his political career.

Samina was right. Men like this had to go. It was the reason we'd entered politics in the first place.

I clenched my fists. God, how stupid was I to play the game with the very people I wanted gone. I let the public think I was a huge supporter of Edgar. I let everyone think I was a modern, more progressive version of the Republican Party but in actuality, I was only a younger form of the same old GOP.

I'd let myself get so caught up in outmaneuvering and winning against my opponents that I'd aligned myself with the enemy who would slit my throat if it meant they'd come out on top. Something that was happening while the good old boys sat back, playing fucking golf.

All of a sudden, an idea came to me. I was going to do what Kimberly suggested. I would call in a favor or two. I wasn't the only one in the party who had issues with Edgar or Decker. Contacting these people would be risky and possibly backfire, but if I could pull it off, neither the president nor any of the Deckers would ever bother me again.

I picked up my phone to dial the person who would help me implement the first step in my plan. However, my phone rang with the tone I'd assigned to Veer. Releasing a sigh, I answered, but before I could say anything, he said, "Jaci. Are you okay?"

His raspy voice washed over me, making me miss him more than ever.

"Veer. I'm sorry."

"You have nothing to be sorry about. The only thing those pictures show is two people who are in love."

I bit my lip and stared out through my window to the DC landscape. He was right—none of the images were dirty in the sense that made politicians' careers end, but they were intimate, showing a side of our relationship we'd shared with no one but each other.

"This could be very bad for Ashur's campaign. Aren't you worried?"

"I'm more worried about you. Edgar is gunning for you. When you helped Tara, you became enemy number one."

"I can handle him. This isn't the first time someone has decided to tarnish my reputation. I'm not going to bring your name into this, but I am going to fight."

The vision of Decker and Edgar on the golf course from the picture in the article flashed behind my eyes. Anger as I'd never felt began to surface.

Did the bastards think I would hide?

"He's dangerous, Jaci." His tone grew to the one that said he would step in to slay my dragons. It made me love him even more. "He will play even dirtier than he has. Right now, he is taking a hands-off approach. If he decided to get personally involved, it could be bad for you."

"I'm a big girl. I've dealt with this kind of thing before."

"This is different, and you know it. He is the damn

president, and he will use his platform to destroy you. Decker's tactics will be child's play compared to Edgar's."

"I signed up for this when I decided to enter politics."

"Dammit, Jaci. I will not let you do anything that will keep you from accomplishing your dreams."

At that moment, Tyler and Samina rushed into my office and came to an abrupt stop. Tyler had a scowl on his face, and Samina crossed her arms while tapping her foot. I lifted my finger to my lips and gestured to the chairs on the other side of my desk.

My back-up team had just arrived. Sam and Ty would understand the path we'd have to take. I hated conducting business like this, but it was necessary.

"If you haven't noticed, I'm linked to you. In my party's eyes, I've already crossed that line."

They tolerated my relationship with Sam because of our family's history, but any romantic entanglement would have them questioning my agenda.

"Now it's time to give them a taste of their own medicine," I continued, causing Sam to lift her brow and a grin to form on her lips.

"For Christ's sake, Jacinta, will you listen to me? You took too many risks as it is when you helped Tara."

"We aren't together anymore, Veer. You have no say in how I handle things."

"As if I ever did," he countered with a tinge of irritation.

I couldn't go down that road. I had enough to deal with than to rehash something that wouldn't make any difference. We'd both made our choices. Although I wasn't the one who wanted to end us. It was him. No, that wasn't fair. I knew what had to happen. Veer only did it before I was ready.

My face must have dropped because Sam set a hand on my arm and squeezed.

"I'll do what is necessary, nothing more. We haven't done anything to be ashamed of. The world will see it soon enough. Tell Ashur I'm sorry. Goodbye, Veer."

I hung up before we continued to go around in circles.

I closed my eyes and waited a few seconds, trying to rein in my emotions. What red-blooded woman didn't want the man she loved to fight for her or try to protect her? The problem was how much I wanted to turn to Veer when I knew I couldn't.

Once I had all the turmoil locked down, I looked up at Tyler and Samina.

"Before either of you jump to follow through on any action running in your heads, I have a plan. One that will put not only Decker in his place but the president as well."

Tyler folded his arms and leaned back in his chair. "I bet I know what it is and she doesn't." He pointed at Samina. "It's a twin thing."

"I bet I do." Sam stuck her tongue out at Tyler. "Your twin routine has nothing on the bond between best friends."

"Yeah, and why's that?"

"Because there is a rule. Sisters before misters." She

nodded at me, and I couldn't help but smile and shake my head.

"I'm her brother. Seriously, Sam, you always get your phrases wrong."

"It's only wrong because you're a boy and wouldn't understand."

"Man."

"What?" she scowled at him.

"I said, I'm a man."

"Says who?"

"My date from last night."

I rolled my eyes, knowing the two stooges routine was to ease the tension I was feeling. God, I loved these two.

"Okay, okay. Neither of you has the inside scoop on this. Especially since I only thought of it a few minutes before you arrived."

"Well, don't keep us waiting." Tyler tapped his watch. "We have reporters circling for comments on your relationships with Veer and Kevin."

"You and everyone else around us will say nothing. I am not going to respond to anything that has to do with my personal life."

I began to write two lists and then handed a paper to each of them. "Here are the people I want you to call. I know they owe you favors. I hate to do this, but we have to play dirty."

Samina cocked her head to the side and watched me. "Jaci, everyone on this list is someone who is teetering on the president's 'Budget of the Century.'" She air-quoted the last part.

"Yes, they are. He needs votes, and I want to make it very difficult for him to get them. I'm going to use the same methods Edgar used against me. A hands-off approach where someone else does the work."

"Hey, are you putting us in the same category as Decker?" Tyler sounded offended.

"No. I'm just making sure I'm squeaky clean while the budget I want to fail more than anything goes up in flames."

"He'll know it was you." Sam tucked the paper into her briefcase.

"That's the point. Edgar will see I'm not a weak peon who will hide from a scandal. And if he fucks with me, we can close bipartisan ranks again and tank anything he sends to Congress. The shit he likes to pull is coming to an end."

"Don't take this the wrong way, Jaci." Tyler leaned forward. "It's about fucking time you figured out you don't need fuckheads like Edgar to win."

I stared at him for a second and realized he hated the fact I'd focused on Edgar to garner support for a future presidential bid.

"I won't make that mistake again. We all make alliances. It's the only way any of us get anything done in DC. But never again will I pretend to follow the pack when I was destined to change it."

Tyler gave me his big, beautiful smile, one that made so

many a debutante flush and fan themselves. "Good, that makes it easier for me to resign from the Advisory Committee. Edgar is about to learn what happens when you mess with the Camdens."

"Now that we got one issue managed, what about Decker?" Sam asked.

"Let's leave that up to Kimberly. Her connections are about to come in handy."

CHAPTER NINETEEN

"SENATOR CAMDEN. May I speak to you a moment?" I heard after I had passed through the security terminals in the United States Capitol Building. The Senate was about to vote on the president's revised spending bill.

Two weeks ago, after Tyler, Sam, and I had met in my office, we began to implement our plan. It started with my father and Tyler resigning from all presidential advisory committees, which had caused a stir with their colleagues and made it obvious the Camdens had closed ranks around me and against Edgar. This in turn had caused the president to demand an investigation into my relationship with Veer, but it was quickly squashed as a ploy to use taxpayer dollars for a personal vendetta, when a tabloid journalist released a recording of the president and Grey Decker Senior plotting the use of any means necessary to ruin my career.

And then our plan continued when Kimberly had

contacted her old college roommate, Cara Decker, a big advocate for helping children and women in crisis, and garnered her support for No Bride. She was another beloved member of the Republican Party and had a lot of influence in Southern politics.

What had come as an unexpected surprise was how vehemently she had distanced herself from her father, Grey Decker Senior. Cara had told Kimberly that she couldn't ignore the actions of the men in her family anymore. There were too many incidences to believe her father and brother were victims of a liberal conspiracy, especially when all of the accusers were members of the GOP.

The final step in our plot had gone into action a few days earlier, when every undecided congressman or woman had been contacted and swayed to vote against the president's bill. Which forced Edgar, the self-proclaimed "president who wouldn't compromise" to adjust his spending allocations to something that would satisfy not only the GOP, but Independents and Democrats as well.

Today's vote would help avoid a government shutdown and show Edgar that I did not need to humiliate him or try to ruin his reputation to make a point. Unlike what he'd done to me. All I needed was the contacts I'd fostered across party lines to tank anything and everything he wanted passed.

I hated playing dirty. It wasn't the way I operated, but when someone backed me into a corner, they'd learn I wasn't the genteel Southern debutante they hoped I was.

They would learn that if they fucked with me I would meet their challenge head-on.

No more treading carefully. It had caused me more pain than it was worth.

I picked up my briefcase from the baggage scanner and turned to find Christopher Robinson walking toward me. "Hi, Chris. What can I do for you?"

He wore a gray pinstriped suit that accentuated the body many designers had fought to clothe. He was the image of a well-tailored businessman.

He glanced at my ring, an antique five-carat diamond surrounded by sapphires that had belonged to Kevin's grandmother, and clenched his jaw. The look in his eyes made me feel self-conscious.

"So, it's true?" He continued to stare at my hand.

I nodded and moved down the hall leading to the Senate chamber. "I'm sure you read about it in the newspapers."

"It's just hard to believe the two of you are getting married, but seeing the ring..." He broke off and grasped the back of his neck.

"For the record, you could have had your chance. I wouldn't have stood in the way. He loves you as I..." It was my turn to trail off.

Shit, I had done a good job of keeping my mind away from Veer, and now seeing Chris, everything was resurfacing.

He touched my arm gently, making me pause my stride, and whispered, "As you love the governor."

I remained quiet, not confirming this statement. If I said anything, my voice would quiver and the resolve I'd built over the last few weeks would crumble.

After a few seconds, I said, "I wanted you two together. Kevin deserves to have happiness."

Chris lifted his gaze to mine. There were dozens of emotions swimming in his eyes. The former model-turned-shipping magnate, in his impeccable clothes, looked as if his world had shattered.

"I wanted to make you an enemy. I wanted you to be the typical small-minded Southern politician, and then I wanted to hate you for loving Kevin and being able to give him the life I refused. He's so loyal to you that I was jealous. I..." He ran a frustrated hand through his hair. "I should have told my family to screw themselves and come out when he wanted to. But I didn't, and now our lives are going in different directions."

"Chris, why are you telling me this? You're engaged to Kathy. She's a wonderful person, who doesn't deserve to be hurt by this. You made a choice. Now you have to accept the consequences."

"She does deserve better. That's why we called it off."

"Say that again?" I'd received a *Save the Date* for Christopher and Kathy's wedding only a week earlier.

It had come during a visit by Kevin. He hadn't taken it well, but this time he hadn't drunk himself into a stupor. Instead, he'd wanted to call a bunch of our friends and go dancing. The both of us had had more fun than we'd anticipated and had ended up pictured in a few tabloids as the up-and-coming "it" couple in DC.

"Kathy and I decided it was better to end our engagement. Just like you, she's always known about my sexuality. She agreed to our arrangement for reasons I won't go into, but in the end, we both realized neither of us would be truly happy together. Our friendship was a hell of a lot more important than family image and expectation."

Holy shit. I'd completely misinterpreted what Kathy knew about Kevin and Chris all along.

I studied Chris. He inhaled deep, as if he was trying to form the right words without offending me. I had a feeling I knew what he was trying to tell me.

Instead of waiting for him to speak, I asked, "Does this mean you want to get back together with Kevin?"

He pinched his lips together, then nodded.

"If Kevin wants you, I'll step aside in a second."

Chris sighed and then closed his eyes, shaking his head. "I tried to call him, but he refused to speak with me. I've left at least thirty messages. I'm desperate and hoped you'd help me."

Refusal was on my lips. However, I held it. Instead, I said, "You ripped Kevin's heart to shreds. He was willing to sacrifice his whole future for you."

At that moment a group of House representatives passed us. We waited until they were at a distance before resuming our conversation.

"I won't let him down again." The determination in his

voice made me soften toward him. He genuinely meant what he said.

However, I wasn't going to help him until I knew what lengths he was willing to go for Kevin.

"I won't let you hurt him again. He deserves someone who will sacrifice as much as he does."

"I told my family."

I cocked my head to the side. "What, exactly, do they know?"

"They know I'm gay. There was no point in mentioning Kevin unless he was willing to..." He paused, gathering his thoughts and then spoke again. "Please help me, Jacinta."

I released a deep breath. "Okay, I'll talk to him tonight after the No Bride fundraiser. His flight doesn't get in until a little before we are to meet, so I can't do it any earlier."

Relief washed over his handsome face. "Thank you."

"But there are no guarantees anything that I have to say will make a difference. Kev is as stubborn as they come."

"Believe me, I know." A halfhearted smile touched his lips. "I want to apologize for what this will cost you if he agrees to take me back."

"It's not as much as you think." My phone beeped, and I checked my watch. "Chris, I have to go. I'm due in the Senate chamber within the next ten minutes."

"Thank you again."

I nodded and moved toward the room I'd spend the next few hours in wishing for a drink.

CHAPTER TWENTY

KEVIN and I walked into the ballroom of Invictus DC a little after eight o'clock in the evening. Deep amber fabric draped the walls of the room, backlit with soft lights. Somehow the bold colors looked elegant and understated instead of gaudy.

Politicians and A-list celebrities clamored around, trying to get the right person's attention, and the approved media were conducting interviews in discreet corners of the room. The bipartisan and public popularity of the No Bride Initiative had made the fundraiser event one of the most coveted invitations to receive. People dressed in their best formal wear, ranging from high-fashion to traditional.

I wore a one-shoulder sapphire gown designed by Shawna Martinez. It was edgy enough to fit with the fashion-conscious Hollywood crowd but conservative enough not to scandalize the stodgiest of politicians.

I glanced over at Kevin, who looked like he'd just

stepped off the runway in his Lanvin shawl-lapel tuxedo. His blond hair was slicked back, giving it a darker hue, and he'd left a light grazing of stubble on his jaw, adding the same fashion edge I was aiming to achieve.

"Kevin, your hotels are better than anything I've ever seen."

"This hotel is my baby. I have to make it the best of all my properties." He grinned with pride.

I could understand his fondness for the place. It was the first project Kevin had invested in that had nothing to do with his family or their money.

"Too bad I have a townhouse in DC, otherwise I'd live in this hotel. But then again, I'd get spoiled by all the pampering."

"That's true, and you already are a handful without adding brat to the mix."

"Hey—" I gave him a light shove, "—not nice."

We walked farther into the room, and I came to an abrupt stop.

Veer stood next to Ashur and Tara, surrounded by people. He was laughing and oozing charm.

I released a deep breath and tried to steady my emotions. Seeing Veer like this, as a candidate for the vice-presidency, made my throat burn. He was a natural, and it was all because he didn't try. My original fear that Veer's non-political, outspoken ways would alienate him from the voters was proven wrong. In fact, Veer's candid nature had made his popularity soar, even with the ultraconservatives of Texas. They saw him as a man who followed up his words with actions, especially since he'd implemented everything he'd promised during the gubernatorial election campaign.

"Are you okay, Jacinta?" Kevin came closer to me and placed a gentle hand on my waist as he turned his gaze in the direction I was looking.

I nodded. "They were meant for this."

Kevin kissed the side of my head. "Yes, they were. No matter what Ashur says, he's not an asshole. Both Ashur and Veer know how to make everyone around them comfortable. They know who they are and don't pretend to be someone else. That's what's made them so popular."

"Unlike us, who have to play certain roles." I was still so angry at myself for aligning with Edgar.

At least I'd learned my lesson and now picked my alliances more carefully.

"They're going to win. I know it." I leaned into Kevin, needing to feel his support.

"It's still too early to know who the leader is for sure, but I agree with you." Kevin ushered me toward a group of GOP constituents.

As I moved into the crowd, my gaze caught Veer's. My heart roared in my ears, and painful sadness engulfed my stomach.

Veer stared at me in that deep, penetrating way that made me feel like he could see to the core of my soul.

The weeks we'd been apart felt like years, and all I wanted was to walk up to him and hug him, to make sure he was okay. But I didn't have the right. I never had, especially not in public.

A painful reminder of another poor decision I'd made.

"I'd suggest you stop looking at him as if he were your lost, stolen puppy, or you're going to add fuel to the rumors and pictures," Kevin said.

My lips trembled, and I nodded. As I glanced away, I noticed Tara and Ashur follow Veer's gaze. Tara placed a hand on Veer's upper arm and then said something. Veer shook his head and turned to face the group around him.

A crushing weight bore down on my chest. It would never be the same between any of us. I'd known it when we parted in New York, but now as two people on opposing political sides, it felt like a giant gulf was between us.

"Let's go, Kev. We only have to be here for another hour, and then we can leave."

Before we could take a step, Kathy and Christopher approached us.

"Jacinta. It's so good to see you," Kathy said and kissed both my cheeks. "You look absolutely beautiful tonight. Is that another of Shawna Martinez's designs?"

I smiled. "Yes, it is."

Kevin stood stiffly next to me and stared at Chris, who was doing the same in return.

I decided to break the tension and leaned into Chris to give him a hug. "How are you, Chris?"

His attention moved to me, and he lifted a brow, asking me without words if I'd talked with Kevin. I gave a slight shake of my head. "I'm good. Kathy wanted to show her support for you and Mrs. Edgar. So, we decided to attend."

"How are you, Kevin?" Kathy asked him. "I miss seeing you. Promise me the next time you're in New York you'll come to see me."

"I promise." Kevin took her hand and brought her in for a light hug. That was when he noticed her finger was missing an engagement ring.

She caught his observation and smiled. "It's exactly what you're thinking, Kev. And I believe you and Christopher need to have a conversation."

Kevin shook his head and pulled out of Kathy's hold and then slipped his arm around me, squeezing my waist tight.

"I wish it were that simple. Some hurts are hard to get over. If you'll excuse us? We have to greet the first lady." Kevin ushered me away before anyone could say another word.

FIVE HOURS LATER, KEVIN HANDED ME A CUP OF TEA and sat down next to me on the steps along the back patio of my DC townhouse.

"There's something I want to talk to you about." I leaned my head against his shoulder.

"If it's about Chris, then save it. He told me where we stood months ago. I refuse to be a consolation."

I ignored his snarky comment. "He came to see me today at the capitol."

"I know. He left a message saying he spoke with you."

I looked up at him and frowned. "Then why the fuck are you sitting here with me and not at the hotel with him?"

"Because I made a promise to you." He lifted my left hand and played with the diamond on my finger.

"That's bullshit, and you know it. If you said you wanted to be with Chris, I'd break the engagement without question. So, cut the crap."

Kevin winced. "What do you want me to say, Jaci? That I don't trust he's telling the truth? Or that I don't believe he will ever come out? His family doesn't even know. I refuse to live a life where I take all the risks and he doesn't."

"He told them," I interjected.

"What?"

I guessed Chris left that part out of his messages to Kevin.

"You heard me. Chris's parents know. Kathy has always known. Now it's up to you."

"Well, fuck." He scratched agitated fingers through his hair, and then looked at me.

Indecision warred on his face. He was one of the best men I had ever encountered. I knew what he was truly worried about now: me. Somehow, I had to convince him that I'd be just fine.

"Jaci, what are we going to do? People are expecting a big white wedding a few weeks after the election."

"You could always use the pictures Decker and Edgar released as the excuse you need to break things off. I can handle the backlash."

In the grand scheme of things, most people had forgotten about the pictures. In the timeframe of pollical scandals, it was a small blip. Americans were more focused on the presidential election than some pictures of a past relationship between two Texas politicians. Hell, a romance movie channel had decided to write a "based on true events" script about two politicians who fell in love. I wouldn't fool myself and think my colleagues had refrained from talking about me behind my back, but that was a small price to pay.

"I'm not going to put you through the wringer any more than you already have."

I set my cup on the step and wrapped my arms around his waist. "You could always come out. Wasn't the stress of hiding your relationship the reason you and Chris broke up? Now there is nothing to stop you from being together."

"It could cost you, in the future. You know some dipshit will spin it that being with you turned me gay." He shook his head. "We have to face it—some people are born assholes."

"You do know I'll support you no matter what you decide? I want you to be happy. You deserve it."

He remained quiet, lost in his thoughts.

After a few moments, he kissed the top of my head and

then threaded his fingers through mine. "I've never had a breakup where I knew without a doubt that my ex would be a genuine friend for the rest of my life."

"Back at you."

A light entered his eyes, something that hadn't been there a few minutes ago.

"Now, we have to fix things with our significant others."

"There is hope for you, love. Not me. I've accepted it. I can't have the White House and the man. It's not in the cards."

"Who says? That man loves you. It's in his eyes. Don't let him go."

"It's too late for us, no matter what I want."

"And people say I'm stubborn."

"Whatever. I'm going to head to bed." I released Kevin's hand and stood.

"I think I'm going to sit out here for a little longer. Maybe make a call or two."

I smiled. "Love you, Kev. Make sure Chris grovels a little before you give in."

"You know I will."

I turned, climbed the steps, and went inside to my cold, empty bed.

CHAPTER TWENTY-ONE

"Senator Camden. We will start in ten minutes."

I nodded and then looked at my reflection in the prep mirror as the makeup artist placed the finishing touches on my face.

It had been exactly thirty days since Kevin and I decided we couldn't do the pretend-couple thing. What surprised me most was the relief I felt. Kevin deserved to live a life he chose instead of one orchestrated for him. Hell, both of us did. Thankfully, our breakup was drowned out by the chaos of election campaigning, nationally and in my state of Texas.

Neither Kevin nor Chris had officially come out, outside of telling their families. For Kevin, the discussion had gone better than expected but not as great as he'd hoped. Kevin was asked to step down from his family's oil business due to him not sharing the company's values. Thankfully, his parents hadn't completely disowned him.

Chris on the other hand, was no longer considered a member of the Robinson family. His parents viewed him as an abomination and wanted nothing to do with him. It broke my heart to think of the pain he must have felt. At least, in the end Kevin and Chris were finally together.

They'd made a handful of public appearances, where a few old-school conservatives had raised their eyebrows, but no one had made any underhanded comments. Well, not to their faces anyway.

My life, on the other hand, was a routine in monotony and self-pity. At least, I had the No Bride Initiative to keep me busy. The first lady and Tara had become the face of the organization, and I assisted in whatever capacity I could between my duties to my constituents and committees.

Work had become the saving grace to keep me from thinking about how lonely my life had become. The only joy I'd had in the last few weeks was when I had the chance to visit Samina, Devin, and my gorgeous nephew in Seattle. Sam was almost ready to deliver a little girl and had decided to limit travel to DC for a while. Spending time with family lessened the loneliness.

I knew I had to start dating again. Sam and Kevin nagged me enough, but I wasn't ready. Plus, seeing Kevin genuinely happy for the first time in years made me realize what a phenomenal mistake I'd made by putting my career and ambition before everything.

I closed my eyes for a brief second, picturing beautiful amber ones gazing at me.

Veer, I miss you so much. Maybe one day we'll find our way back to each other.

I knew my thoughts were wishful thinking, but I needed something to hold on to.

"Senator, we're ready."

I stood, letting the stylist take the smock covering my clothes, and walked toward the soundstage, taking my seat next to Candice McDavers. She was an ultraconservative radio and television personality in Texas, who had no qualms about getting down to the nitty gritty. She had a reputation for ruffling feathers, especially with the good old boys of Southern politics, something I couldn't help but love about her. She'd invited me to visit the next time I returned home to Austin and so I took her up on her offer. Today's interview would be the perfect stage to discuss the highlights of the No Bride Initiative. With any luck, she wouldn't question me about the election or the pictures.

Who was I kidding? Those would be the first things she asked about.

The stage signal turned from red to green, indicating we were on air.

"Senator Camden, thanks for joining us today. Before we discuss your work with No Bride, I wanted to start with your opinion on last night's third presidential debate. The polls show Ashur Kumar as the clear winner against President Henry Edgar and Democrat Baron Johnson. What are your thoughts?"

And I was right. Candace knew a story and I'd given the media plenty to chew over.

"It is hard to have an unbiased opinion when two of the men are friends of mine."

I could almost hear Samina chanting "Liar, Liar" in my ear.

"You're referring to the president and Mr. Kumar?"

"Yes, both are strong men who made valid points. They both represent the conservative values our nation needs." I paused, knowing what I said next would ruffle a few feathers. I was finished playing a game where pompous assholes threatened me into falling in line. "However, I must agree with the polls. The president missed opportunity after opportunity to show how he will refocus his agenda to one that would benefit most Americans, if not all. Instead of turning around the negative views of his presidency, he emphasized why the majority of Americans disapprove of his performance in the White House."

A flash of surprise crossed Candice's face. The public still thought the president favored me, and not throwing my complete support behind him wouldn't go unnoticed by her or the audience.

Candice recovered quickly and then asked, "Could you give the audience an example?"

I nodded. "On the issue of veterans' benefits. By personally attacking a decorated war veteran like Kumar on his service record, the president missed a chance to show the voters he understood the sacrifice the men and women of the military make every day. He was so focused on tearing Ashur Kumar's reputation that he never answered the question about what he would do to improve the benefits crisis plaguing the military health care system. His stance made him look as if he couldn't relate."

"So, what you're saying is that since the president has never experienced combat, he shouldn't have an opinion?"

I wanted to glare, but I kept calm. "No, I'm saying that as the leader of our military, he needed to show his support for those who have put their lives on the line instead of criticizing them."

A roar of applause broke out.

"Would your passionate response be due to the fact you are working with the future Mrs. Kumar on the No Bride Initiative?"

"My work with Tara Zain has the full support of the first lady. It is a bipartisan project that seeks to end child enslavement and the practice of child brides. My work with Tara has nothing to do with American politics and everything to do with saving lives."

"I agree. That is, after all, why you are with us today. Let's discuss the details of what has become the first lady's pet project."

I almost sighed in relief. The last thing I wanted to do was talk Ashur, because I knew, without a doubt, it would lead to questions about the pictures of Veer and me.

It took another fifteen minutes of discussion before the inevitable question arose. I knew better than to hope I'd escaped the inquiry into my relationship with Veer.

"I can't end this without discussing the pictures of you and Governor Veer George."

My hands shook slightly before I wrestled them under control. Candice watched me, analyzing every microscopic detail about me.

"With the recent end of your engagement, many of us are curious if your relationship with the governor was the cause and if you two are a couple or just friends?"

I squared my shoulders and stared into the camera pointed in my direction. "Governor George was not the reason Kevin and I decided marriage wasn't best for us. Our reasons for breaking up are private, and we remain the closest of friends."

"What about the governor? What is the status of your relationship? The pictures posted a few weeks ago say you are more than friends."

"Those were private moments leaked by people who are intimidated by a woman in power. I'm not ashamed to admit Veer George and I had an intimate relationship in the past. What better person to fall in love with than someone who is your best friend?"

"Does that mean you two are a couple?"

I shook my head, and I kept my face emotionless, holding in tears and the pain as I'd trained myself to do over the past few weeks. "We parted ways to pursue our different ambitions."

Her eyes softened, telling me she saw past the polished image I displayed. This reporter was a barracuda who wasn't easy on anyone. I guessed she felt sorry for me.

"Some would say you have the same ones—after all, he is the vice-presidential candidate."

"I won't deny that my goal is to one day hold the highest office in the country, but it's not my time. I'm a junior senator who is barely thirty-two. In a few more years, I'll be ready."

"Thank you, Senator Camden. Please come back again."

Once we were given the signal that we were off air, I stood, letting the production assistant take off my microphone, and then I moved toward Trisha, who waited for me off set.

"Senator Camden."

I turned.

"Can I ask you one last question, off the record?"

I nodded and braced myself for whatever Candice was about to ask. Anything off the record would mean it was something personal. At this point, I was too raw to hide anything.

Candice remained quiet for a second and then asked, "You are poised to be the frontrunner for your party in four years, no matter who wins this year's election. Would you give it up if he asked you to?"

We both knew the "he" she referred to was Veer.

"Yes," I answered, not thinking twice that nosy media personnel surrounded me. It wasn't as if it would make a difference. Then I added, "But he would never ask me to do that. He's too good of a man to make me pick him over my dreams."

Veer and I were over. I'd accepted the fact my ambition had ruined what we had. I knew it was time to move on.

She responded with another question, but I'd started walking.

"Let's meet tomorrow morning. I'm exhausted and want a night alone," I said to Trisha as I approached her.

With a nod and a weary smile, she gave me my handbag. She'd watched the interview and understood the hole I'd created. No doubt party leaders were going to ream me as soon as they heard what I'd said. I'd all but endorsed Ashur's ticket.

At this point, I couldn't give a damn what anyone thought. Ashur and Veer were men of integrity who'd done more for our country as children of immigrants than those whose families had lived in the US for generations.

I took the elevator down and stepped out the doors before they could completely open. The cool breeze mixed with the light fall heat and clung to my sensitive skin, giving slight ease to the turmoil churning inside my being. However, with each step I took toward my car, the weight of my loss weighed down on my shoulders. By the time I entered the limousine, I was on the verge of sobbing.

I waited for the car to move before I let go of my emotions. First, a whimper escaped, then a loud sob.

I covered my face with my hands and cried as I hadn't cried before. Even after my attack, I hadn't felt this much pain.

Everything I ever wanted was within grasp, and the one thing I needed was completely out of reach.

What kind of idiot was I to let the love of my life go because of our party lines? If only I'd compromised some, there may have been a chance for us. Now if Ashur won, Veer and I would be separated by a huge political wall. He'd marry someone else, have children with someone else, live a life with someone else.

I covered my empty womb with my hand and cried even harder. I couldn't imagine having a baby with anyone but Veer.

I rocked back and forth, lost in my grief and sorrow. Fifteen minutes later, when my car pulled through the gates of my estate, I had myself under some semblance of control.

Hiccupping, I stepped out of the car, and in a numb haze, I entered my big, empty house. I scanned the single place setting on the island designed to serve a large family and winced.

This pitiful existence was my life.

I reached for my cell phone, thinking a call to Sam would cheer me up, but pulled back. I couldn't call her. She was already in the middle as it was. Veer was hers as much as I was. Plus, she was probably asleep by now anyway.

I moved toward the back hallway of the house and descended the stairs to the wine cellar. Picking out a bottle of my favorite Bordeaux, I poured myself an extra-large serving and drank down half the glass, letting the smooth liquid dull my senses.

I made my way to my bedroom, kicking off my heels and setting my drink on the bedside table. Stripping my clothes into a pile, I walked into the bathroom, turned on the shower to the hottest setting my body could handle, and then stepped into the scalding spray.

The water beat down on me, seeping into my tense muscles. I leaned my head against the shower wall, feeling defeated and alone.

My ambition came at a price, and now I had to live with it.

I'd set myself up for a perfect political future. A future I didn't want without the one man who made my heart skip a beat with his not-quite-perfect smile.

I closed my eyes and let out a whimper, feeling another wave of sadness bear down on me. After a few more minutes of self-pity, I shook my head and smacked the tile of the shower.

"I'm such a goddammed idiot!" I shouted. "This is not how my story with Veer will end."

I refused to believe there was not hope. I had to find him and tell... What the hell was I going to tell him?

My shoulders sagged for a second and then the idea came to me. He was due back at his house tonight. I'd go there and wait for him. Hopefully, he'd forgive me for my stupidity and would be willing to give us another chance. I'd tell him I'd wait as long as it took to make my dreams come true as long as he was with me.

Maybe then, he'd understand that he meant more to me than anything else.

"Time to go all in, Jacinta." I released a deep breath and turned, coming to an abrupt stop.

Veer stood before me in all his naked glory.

I blinked the water from my eyes, trying to make sure I wasn't imagining him in my shower.

I reached out and my fingers pressed against his hard chest.

"I'm really here, baby." He covered my hand with his and stepped forward, but I held him back. Water glided down his golden muscled arms and chest.

"What are you doing here?"

"I heard your interview."

"I wasn't going to trash you."

"I never thought you would." He paused, and his gaze bored into mine. "I also heard about what you said to Candice McDavers after."

Wincing, I released a sigh.

"That was off the record." I knew it was going to get out but hadn't expected it to be so fast.

His lips curved in the way that brought butterflies into my stomach. "You should know by now nothing is off the record, especially when you're in a studio with high-definition microphones."

"It doesn't matter what my answer was. I'm not sure it will change anything." I wiped the spray from my face and tried to push Veer back so I could move past him and not feel so exposed, so vulnerable.

Veer wouldn't budge, and the heat of his hot skin burned through my fingertips.

"It changes everything. You want me."

"I never said otherwise."

"I want you, Jaci."

"That was never our problem. Sex was the one place we never, ever had issues. But..."

"But?"

"I don't just want sex. I want more." My hand curled against the crisp hair on his chest, loving the feel of him under my fingertips.

"How much more?"

There was an intensity to his eyes that confirmed he wanted me, and the low hum that constantly pulsed inside me woke with a boom.

Fuck. Focus, Jacinta. Sex is not the answer.

I couldn't get distracted. I had to get my words out before I lost my nerve. Although, naked was not how I planned to confess my feelings.

I guessed beggars couldn't be choosers and began to speak. "Ever since I was little, all I ever dreamed about was a political career. The idea of being the first female president consumed me."

"I know, Jaci," Veer interjected, keeping the distance my arm provided. "Why do you think I ended it between us? I couldn't stand between you and your dreams. You were born for this. You were raised to play the game and win."

"What if I said I don't want the dream or to win without you?" I tried to turn around so he couldn't see my uncertainty. "None of it matters, if you're not there with me."

Veer stopped me by pressing his body to the front of mine and tilting my face up. His gaze penetrated mine.

"What to repeat that?"

I swallowed down that lump in my throat. "I...I don't want to do this without you anymore. I know, I made you feel like you were second and I can't make excuses for what I did. All I can do is ask you to forgive me." My lips trembled and Veer's thumb ran over them. "I'll wait until you and Ash finish your terms. I'll wait for the nomination. Hell, I'll wait forever, if it means we are together. My ambition means nothing, if it means I'm half alive."

"When did you come to this conclusion?" His voice was cool, almost emotionless, except his touch was so tender as he ran a hand down my side.

"I've thought about barely anything else for the last few weeks."

"Our relationship could cost you more than you can imagine. Not only a future nomination but reelection to the Senate."

I lifted my chin. "I'm willing to risk it."

He remained quiet for what felt like hours, watching me, studying me. Then just as my shoulders sagged, and the tears I thought I'd spent reappeared, Veer said, "I want the dream with you too."

I exhaled the breath I hadn't realized I held.

"Really?" A tear slipped down my cheek as Veer cupped my face.

"I want you by my side, Jaci. I don't want any of this

without you either." Before I could respond, he continued, "But know this, I won't ever let you give up your dream. Even if it is twenty years from now. You will be up on that podium taking the highest office in the nation."

I stared at him through water-misted lashes. My heart drummed in a deafening beat, and my lips trembled.

"A relationship with me could make you lose the election too. I represent a lot of what you and Ashur oppose. No matter what my personal stance may be, people will only see what the GOP has historically done."

He moved forward, pressing me against the tile-covered wall of the giant shower. The crisp hair on his chest rubbed against my nipples. "It's a risk I'm willing to take."

"Have you talked to Ashur about this? It's his ticket you're running on."

"I wouldn't worry about him."

I frowned. "Of course I'm going to worry about him. He's leading in the polls by over thirty points. I won't be the cause of a rift between you two."

Veer cupped my breast and rolled my nipple with his thumb, making me lose my concentration.

"He's the one who sent me the recording of the interview and your off-the-record conversation."

"What?" I grabbed his hand, but that only made him squeeze harder.

"You heard me. Ash wants us together. He knows you're the one who helped Tara with the incident overseas.

He wants to pay it forward, and he couldn't care less if it costs him the election. It's not as if the two of us don't have jobs if we lose."

Hope bloomed inside my body.

"What do you say, Jaci? Ready to turn the political circuit on its ass?"

For the first time in months, I felt the tug of happiness enter my body, and I leaned into Veer, smiling. "Yes."

"Good." There was a roughness to his voice that told me he was being filled with the same overload of emotions I was.

I stood on tiptoes and kissed his forehead. Veer gripped my nape with his other hand and tilted it up. Water dripped from his hair and down the side of his beautiful face.

"Just so you know, I came here with the intention of begging you to keep me, but you beat me to it."

"Well, I guess you can't win them all."

"True, true." His eyes lit up, and a wide grin touched his lips. "You know what this means?"

I couldn't help but smile up at him. "What?"

"You're going to have lots of politically hybrid babies with a liberal."

"Is that right?"

"Yes. I may even convince you to come over to the dark side."

"I love you, but it won't make me change my views."

"Say that again." His tone grew soft and his gaze intensified.

I ran my thumb down the scar on his cheek, across his lips, and then leaned up to kiss him.

"I love you, Veer George. Let's make some politically hybrid babies."

"I suggest we start this very moment."

EPILOGUE

Veer and I entered Ashur's Houston campaign headquarters to cheers and shouts. Banners, American flags, and confetti filled the room, as did the incredible number of supporters. Tara and Ashur smiled when they saw us, waving at us to join them.

The two of them had grown into a level of tolerance for each other that never betrayed that the true nature of their relationship was a business deal. What they seemed oblivious to was the sexual tension that floated around them whenever they were in a room. The media loved to comment on the chemistry between them and how they couldn't wait for their large wedding.

Veer loved to make sly comments about how Ashur watched his fiancée as a man ready to lick every inch of her, fuck her, or do both. Which would result in a "fuck off" or a scowl. Tara, on the other hand, could handle

Ashur's presence with cold indifference, something I knew was a complete front.

As we made our way down the walkway, various campaign staffers hugged us. There was a spirit of victory in the room, even though nothing was official. The last of the voting polls

were near closing with the Kumar-George ticket in the clear lead. Once California came in, there was no going back. Ashur would become the next President of the United States.

We stepped onto the stage to another round of cheers. Veer stepped in the direction of where Ashur stood, but then turned back to me.

"Wish me luck." Veer tucked a lock of hair behind my ear and kissed my forehead.

"No luck needed, soon-to-be former Governor George. You have this in the bag."

He snorted. "You're too confident, Senator Camden-George."

I smiled. Two months ago, we'd married in an intimate wedding on my parents' estate in Louisiana. My heart seemed to skip a beat whenever I thought about marrying the man I loved and the possibility of still achieving the future I'd planned for since childhood. I knew nothing was guaranteed, but there was still a chance. Of course, there were grumblings about my rekindled relationship with Veer. However, I couldn't give two shits what the old boys' club thought.

"It's not confidence, baby. It's a sure thing." I gripped the lapel of his suit.

Veer's face grew concerned for a split second. "This means you'll have to wait a little longer."

"Maybe not. I could decide to run against Ashur and you in four years," I teased.

He lifted a brow and then smiled. "That should keep our marriage interesting."

"But then again, if Ashur is the kind of president I think he'll be, it'll be well worth the wait to get the endorsement of a popular president *and* my party."

Samina had put that little idea in my head a few weeks earlier, and I couldn't help but agree with her. Now it was all about patience and continuing in my role as senator from the great state of Texas.

Veer shook his head. "Don't ever change, Jaci."

"You never have to worry about that." I stood on tiptoes and kissed him. "Now go join Ashur—he's waiting. And then later tonight, the senator from Texas is going to screw the new vice-president's brains out."

A sexy gleam lit his eyes. "I look forward to it, Senator."

THE END

Commander

Coming September 20, 2018
Pre-Order Here —>> https://amzn.to/2KY648k

I am Tara Zain.

Human rights attorney, the Commander to my colleagues in international affairs, and fiancé to the most powerful man in the country.

I've learned love is a useless distraction. Money and status are the true motivators, and powerful alliances are much more important than romantic entanglements. My passion is my work, and nothing, not even the promise of happily-ever-after, will keep me from accomplishing my mission.

This is why I've made a bargain with the one man who shattered my heart years ago. He's proposed that I stand by his side and foster the beginning of a new political dynasty.

But I have secrets.

Secrets that could destroy not only this man and the passion we've rekindled but the very laws of the nation he has sworn to uphold.

I am Tara Zain. Future First Lady of the United States of America and COMMANDER.

94384516R00156

Made in the USA
Middletown, DE
19 October 2018